I0817964

ONLY MURDER

(A Sadie Price FBI Suspense Thriller—Book 1)

Rylie Dark

Rylie Dark

Debut author Rylie Dark is author of the SADIE PRICE FBI SUSPENSE THRILLER series, comprising three books (and counting) and the CARLY SEE FBI SUSPENSE THRILLER, comprising three books (and counting).

An avid reader and lifelong fan of the mystery and thriller genres, Rylie loves to hear from you, so please feel free to visit www.ryliedark.com to learn more and stay in touch.

ISBN: 978-1-0943-9279-0

BOOKS BY RYLIE DARK

SADI PRICE FBI SUSPENSE THRILLER
ONLY MURDER (Book #1)
ONLY RAGE (Book #2)
ONLY HIS (Book #3)

CARLY SEE FBI SUSPENSE THRILLER
NO WAY OUT (Book #1)
NO WAY BACK (Book #2)
NO WAY HOME (Book #3)

CHAPTER ONE

There was no one around.

He loved this time in the morning, when the silence was as all-encompassing as the ice that covered everything in sight, and the sky still a heavy indigo that made vision impossible without his head-torch. It was at least an hour before dawn and he was the only fisherman on the lake, which was the way that Tom Willoughby preferred it.

He found an odd comfort in the quiet, or perhaps not so odd considering that he shared his home with a talkative wife and daughter and two endlessly chattering grandchildren. The frozen lake and pre-dawn darkness had become his escape. Surrounded by nothing but ice and pine-covered mountains, this was a harsh and unforgiving landscape. Yet to him, it was the most beautiful place in the world.

Tom hummed softly to himself as he went through the same prepping routine that he had for years; getting the hole squared away, baiting the hooks, and ensuring that the rods and reels were in the perfect position. It was a routine that had become second nature to him now, requiring little in the way of conscious thought, and his set up was soon complete. All he had to do now was wait.

Ice-fishing could be a laborious and sometimes thankless task, but Tom was one of the best. He knew the ideal times to fish and the best spots, and where one could find a good shoal of arctic char, the biggest pikes, and even a few land-locked salmon. It had been a while since he had brought home a tasty haul of salmon. Tom knew the art of being quiet too, unlike some of the tourists who visited here, with their shiny new gear and expensive snow boots, eager for a try at getting a good yield from the frozen lakes.

Tom was lost in thought when one of his lines snagged and snapped him to attention. With a practiced urgency he began to reel in his catch, only to find the rod bowing and his back bending under the weight of it. He felt a thrum of excitement; whatever this was, it was big, even bigger than the huge pike he had caught five years ago now, which had been the talk of the whole of Anchorage.

Just like that pike, this one didn't want to be caught and the heavy resistance strained his muscles and caused sweat to break out on his brow. As he wrestled with the creature on the end of his hook, the rod threatening to spring from his hands, Tom wondered if it was a fish that he had caught at all. There was no fight to it, no desperate pulling to wrench itself free. It felt like a dead weight.

As he dragged it towards the hole, his muscles corded with tension and Tom felt a sense of foreboding begin to take shape as it came closer.

That sense was realized as his catch finally came into view, emerging from the hole's surface, blue and bloated with a strange sheen to its waxy skin.

Tom knew a dead thing when he saw it, and his eyes strained to see what kind of animal carcass his hook had made its home in. What poor creature had gotten trapped underneath the frozen lake until he had dragged it back to the light?

Then he saw the long strands of dark hair and his stomach hurled. He shouted instinctively for help even though he knew there was no one around to hear him, and suddenly the silence didn't seem comforting at all.

CHAPTER TWO

"Jessica!"

Sadie screamed as she ran down the hill, skidding on the ice as she did so. Behind her, her friends called for her to come back, to not look, but Sadie felt hope filling her even though she somehow already knew it was futile.

Jessica had been missing for three days in the middle of a winter that was harsh even for the hinterlands. If it was indeed her sister that they were fishing out of the frozen lake at the bottom of the hill, then there was no way that she could still be alive.

Yet still, Sadie hoped.

Jessica couldn't be gone. Her older sister was her rock, the person she relied on, and the one who shielded her from their father's drunken rages which for some reason always seemed to be directed straight at Sadie. After a few drinks, he blamed Sadie for everything.

He would find a way to blame her for this, too. He always did.

The flicker of hope changed to despair as Sadie reached the bottom of the hill and ran to the lake. A crowd of onlookers had gathered, watching to see what – or who – the Dive and Search team had found. Faces turned her way as she approached, and she heard a murmur ripple through the crowd.

She heard the pity in their voices even before she could make out what they were saying, and that was when she knew. Really knew.

Jessica was gone. But the body they were pulling out of the lake, which she could see now, couldn't be her sister. Underneath the blue tinge and the bloating, it might look like her, it might have her long dark hair, but it wasn't Jessica. A frozen pile of flesh could not be her vibrant, beautiful sister. Perhaps it had housed her once, but Jessica was no longer there.

Someone stepped in front of her, hands outstretched, preventing her from getting any closer.

"Sadie, sweetheart," she recognized the voice of one of her father's friends, "stay here. You don't want to see her like this."

"It's not Jessica," she said stubbornly, trying to push her way past. Hands gripped her arms. There were other adults surrounding her now, speaking to her in hushed tones that infuriated her. She struggled against them. A State Trooper walked towards her, his face etched with the same pity as the others.

"Let me go!" she screamed. She didn't want to talk to him, to any of them. She didn't want to hear it.

A loud sobbing noise came from somewhere, a sound that seemed to echo around the lakes, disembodied from its source. It took Sadie a while before she realized that it was coming from her.

She crumpled then, sinking to the floor and into the soft snow. Someone's arms went around her, but Sadie pushed them away. Someone was talking to her, trying to soothe her. Telling her that everything was going to be all right.

Sadie knew that they were lying.

Nothing was going to be all right ever again.

*

Sadie jolted awake, looking wildly around and expecting to see the lake and the crowd of people, confused when she saw that she was inside a taxicab.

It was just a dream, she told herself as she breathed deeply, trying to calm her racing heartbeat. *Just a dream.*

It had been a long time since she had experienced those dreams. Glimpses from a past that she had worked hard to file away in her memory.

But now she was driving straight back into it.

Sadie saw the taxi driver looking at her in the rearview mirror, his eyes concerned. She hoped that she hadn't been thrashing about or talking in her fractured sleep.

It had been nine hours since the taxicab had picked her up from the airport at Juneau, and apart from a few toilet breaks there had been no chance to stretch her legs. Before her dream, she had tried to sleep on and off, only to jerk awake as her head knocked against the window and she was reminded of where she was and where she was going.

Home.

It was funny, but it didn't feel like home at all.

The Alaskan landscape stretched on for miles on either side of her, the snow-covered mountains towering over her and making her feel so much smaller than she had in the city. The pitch black of night had given way to the dull gray of early morning and her surroundings were starting to take shape. At this time of the year the whole place was covered in different shades of white, from the deceptively fluffy looking blankets of snow that covered the evergreens to the blue-white mountain tips above her. It was both familiar and strange, a different world from the one she had been used to in the decade since she had left.

On either side of the road, snowbanks twice her own height hemmed them in. There were few other cars on the road that morning, other than the odd snow truck and another, lone taxicab going in the opposite direction. Leaving Anchorage just as Sadie was returning.

Unlike her, the landscape hadn't changed. Long after she was gone, the same mountains would be here, looking down impassively at the travelers below, unimpressed by their comings and goings. As impervious to Sadie's return as they had been the day that she had left, vowing never to set eyes on them again.

Unlike many who left Alaska though, it hadn't been the unforgiving landscape or the harsh climate that had prompted her departure.

Although it wasn't cold inside the cab, Sadie shivered and pulled her coat tighter around herself as though she could prevent the memories from assailing her. The closer that she got to her childhood home, the clearer they became. Why had she thought that the passage of time would make them any easier to bear? Not for the first time, she questioned her decision to return. To escape to the first place that she had ever needed to escape from.

"Nearly there now, ma'am," the driver said gruffly, cutting into her thoughts. Sadie murmured a thank you, taking her eyes off the mountains and the ice and looking ahead as they started to approach something resembling civilization again.

They turned off the main road into the city and the snowbanks and evergreen-covered peaks became a backdrop to rows of gray buildings and scattered local businesses. A man on a dog sled crossed the road in front of them and the taxicab driver tutted with annoyance, no doubt in a hurry to drop Sadie off and get some sleep.

She was reminded suddenly of driving along this very road with her dad, heading into the town center to do a monthly shop, stocking up on goods to see them through a winter that had been harsher than this one. Not that Alaskan winters were ever anyone's idea of mild.

He had been shouting at her, his knuckles white as they gripped the steering wheel, spit flying from his ranting mouth to hit the dashboard in front of him. Sadie couldn't remember what he had been shouting about, but it didn't matter. He was always shouting.

Especially at her. Somehow, everything had always been Sadie's fault, in her father's eyes at least.

They pulled up outside the square, brown building of the Anchorage FBI Field Office, and Sadie let out a breath she only then became aware that she was holding. She was here, at her new base. The implications of her decision to transfer all the way to Alaska from DC suddenly felt very real to Sadie, but she squared her shoulders, pulled up her hood and scarf, and reminded herself that her decision had been the right one, before she opened the cab door to step outside onto High Street, the muscles in her legs protesting after hours of being static in the cab.

Sadie gasped as the cold hit her like a slap.

She had expected it, of course, but had forgotten that here, in the depths of Alaska, the word *cold* carried very different connotations than it had down south. Especially in midwinter. This was a bone-deep numbness that left frost on her eyelashes, in spite of the furry hood that she wore and the thick scarf that was wrapped around her face. The back of her throat froze with every inhalation as she took her case from the cab driver and thanked him for his service.

It wasn't just physical, either. The shock of the temperature after the warmth inside the taxicab seemed to chill her very thought processes and it took a few minutes for Sadie to collect herself before she headed into the office to find an empty reception.

Stamping her feet on the plastic grid that served as a welcome mat to get the snow off her boots, Sadie took her first look around the Field Office for Anchorage.

It was a lot smaller and shabbier than she was used to, a far cry from the shining and polished halls of the headquarters at DC. There, Sadie had been one of hundreds of people milling about, all with an air of importance as they went about federal business. This place was almost eerily quiet, and a layer of dust seemed to cling to every available surface. Her certainty about her decision flickered for a moment as she looked around and realized what she had left behind.

Anchorage had been regarded as a dead end down south, in terms of career progression, but Sadie knew that was no reflection on the caliber of the agents. Alaskans were rugged, resilient people in Sadie's experience, and she was under no illusions that this would be an easy post, although quieter than she had previously been used to.

That quiet, she reminded herself, was why she had requested it. Alaska was what her mother had always referred to as a 'place of the edges,' and with the never-ending whiteness that stretched on up to the Arctic Ocean, it had always felt like the edge of the world to Sadie.

Then, of course, there were the people. 'Edgy' was a good description. As well as the hardy endurance of the natives, the fishermen and the oil-rig workers, there were those who had moved here from other places, seeking the silence and the snow. Misfits, usually, or outlaws. People running away from something.

Sadie thought that maybe she would fit right back in.

"Can I help you?"

A young field agent came through an adjoining door into the reception area, bright blue eyes looking suspiciously at Sadie. She pulled her badge out from under the thick confines of her jacket.

"Special Agent Price, reporting for duty," Sadie said and watched the respect gleam in the other agent's eyes. He looked young and freshly qualified, without the jaded look that all agents got eventually.

Give him time, Sadie thought. Her ten years on the job were enough to leave anyone jaded. He practically bounced over to shake her hand, which was still encased in her padded gloves. She couldn't imagine ever feeling warm enough to take them off.

"Field Agent O'Hara," he said. Sadie noticed the wispy stubble on his chin. "We will be working together at some point, I'm sure."

Sadie smiled politely, not wanting to burst the younger agent's bubble by telling him that, wherever possible, she preferred to work alone. These days, anyway.

O'Hara must have been expecting a more enthusiastic response as his smile dimmed slightly. "Right, I'll take you through," he said. Sadie followed him back through the door he had entered and down the corridor to the office of the ASAC, or Assistant Special Agent-in-Charge. Anchorage wasn't big enough to warrant an Assistant Director, even though it covered the whole state.

Sadie had done her homework before arriving, and she knew that the ASAC, Paul Golightly, was a veteran agent with decades in the field. Originally from Ketchikan, he had stayed put in Alaska his whole life, stubbornly refusing transfers to other states even though Sadie suspected he would have been able to achieve a higher rank if he had done so.

Suddenly nervous, she wondered how she would be received, and how Golightly would feel about one of Quantico's finest pitching up at his office. She had been so focused on getting away from her old post that she had given little thought to the new one, including her new colleagues. Now though, she felt her palms go clammy with anticipation.

Golightly's cool gray eyes appraised her as she entered his office. He was a small, wiry man in his late fifties, although he looked older, with deep wrinkles splitting his leathery cheeks. He waved Sadie into a seat.

"O'Hara," he barked, "fetch Agent Price a hot drink, would you?"

"I'm fine, thank you, I had plenty to drink on the drive here," Sadie said. At each services stop she had ordered the strongest coffee they served, and she doubted if she would get any sleep that night with the level of caffeine in her system.

O'Hara left the room, shutting the door behind him, and Golightly steepled his hands under his chin and looked at Sadie until she started to feel awkward.

"Welcome to Anchorage," he said eventually. "You come highly recommended."

"Thank you, Sir."

"So, what I'm wondering," he went on, "is why a BAU hotshot like yourself is being transferred to a bumfuck place like Alaska?"

Sadie swallowed, feeling the tension rise in her throat. She had expected the question and already knew what her answer would be. It was giving away more of her background than she was entirely comfortable with, but it would deflect from the full story about Jessica and, besides, it would come out sooner or later.

"I am Alaskan," she said simply. "I moved away years ago. I saw the opening for the post, and decided it was time to come home."

The last word sounded odd to her own ears. Alaska hadn't been home for a long time, during most of which she had sworn that she would never come back.

"Fair enough," Golightly said, and Sadie was relieved when he didn't seem inclined to press any further.

"That's a relief, Agent, because it means you will be used to the way things are here. To me, Alaska is the best place in the world to be, but there's many who can't cope with the cold and the ice. The job can be quiet for months. We've had five agents in your post in the last four years."

Sadie wasn't too surprised, and she doubted that the reason was solely about the climate, although it no doubt played a big enough part. Less big cases to solve meant less chance for promotion.

Golightly picked up a piece of paper from the desk in front of him, and Sadie spotted her name. It was her resumé, no doubt sent through from DC. The ASAC skimmed through it, nodding and grunting in approval here and there. Then he looked up, his eyebrows raised in admiration.

"You were on that Boston serial killer case? The one that used power tools on his victims? That was in the news for months. Heck, even up here, folks were talking about it."

"Yes," Sadie nodded. "I was the BAU agent assigned to that case."

Golightly looked impressed. "I heard it was the behavioral analysis expert that cracked it. You did good."

Sadie, never easy with compliments, tried not to squirm in her seat. She knew that her resume was good, better than good in fact. It cast her in a glowing light. There was nothing on the neatly typed page that revealed the intricacies of Sadie's last big case, the one that had nearly broken her. The one that had driven her all the way up here, to what could easily be a career dead end.

When he had finished, Golightly fixed her with that searching look again, peering at her over the desk.

"You must be pretty darn fond of the place to come back," he said. Sadie swallowed, hoping that he wasn't going to ask too many questions, even though she knew that he must have plenty of them.

"Folks work hard for years to get in the Behavioral Analysis Unit," he continued, and Sadie's stomach sank as she heard the note of suspicion in his voice. "Seems pretty odd to me that anyone would leave it to come back here. Can't say as we've ever had a BAU agent here before."

"I guess it was just time to come home," Sadie said quietly. She looked down, feeling Golightly's eyes still boring into her, and the tension in the small office was suddenly palpable, as though all the words that she was speaking were vibrating in the air around them.

"I suppose everyone goes home, eventually," Golightly added, barely disguising the curiosity in his voice. Sadie didn't answer. She wasn't sure that the ASAC would welcome her primary motive for returning to Alaska, the thing that had driven her whole career, if she dared to be honest with herself.

Sadie had gotten good at catching killers, but there was one that she still had left to apprehend.

Her sister's.

"Well, we don't get too many psycho killers up here either," Golightly said, oblivious to the dark turn in Sadie's thoughts. "Not too many lunatics running around with power tools."

"I've had my fill of them," Sadie said lightly, attempting a smile. There was a silence, then Golightly sat back in his seat and the tension in the air between them softened.

"You're staying in town?" he asked, clearly deciding to drop the subject for the time being. Sadie nodded, relief washing over her.

"I've got a motel room booked less than half a mile away. I figured the closer the better with the travel conditions in the winter. I have a few rental places to view over the next few weeks, all local."

"Good. Will you be calling in on any old friends while you're here? It can be a lonely place when you don't know anyone. You've been outside Alaska a long time."

"I'm from up in the hinterlands, just up from the Nancy Lakes area," Sadie said, her mouth dry. Coming across familiar faces from her past was not something that she was looking forward to. "A lot of my school friends moved away; I think."

Golightly shrugged. "A lot of folks do. Okay, Price, go and get yourself settled in. I'll see you here at eight am sharp tomorrow morning."

Sadie was standing up to leave when O'Hara came in, his previously eager face now grim. Sadie felt a familiar stirring in her stomach; something had happened and, judging by the look on O'Hara's face, it was going to involve a body bag or two.

But nothing could have prepared her for the young agent's next words.

"There's been a body found up in the lakes, Sir," he said. Golightly raised bushy, gray eyebrows.

"Not a lot of information you're giving me there, O'Hara. Male, female? I'm assuming there's suspicion of foul play if we've been notified."

O'Hara blushed as he replied. "Sorry Sir. Female, early twenties, as yet unidentified. The Medical Examiner is with the body now at the site. All I know is there are possible indications of forced drowning. I don't have any more information than that. She was found in the early hours of the morning by an ice-fisherman named Tom Willoughby. He reeled her in." O'Hara grimaced at the image.

"Which lakes?" Golightly asked.

"Up at Nancy," O'Hara said. "Part of the Lynx Lake Loop."

The Lynx lakes consisted of at least fourteen lakes, which spent a large part of the year completely frozen and so were popular with both ice skaters and ice fishermen. They were all connected, a large body of water fed by a gorge a few miles north of the area.

Jessica had been found in those same lakes.

Sadie stared at O'Hara, trying to hide the sudden surge of adrenaline, but Golightly must have noticed her reaction, as he looked at Sadie with a challenge in his eyes.

"Well, what do you know? This is an omen if ever I saw one. A potential murder on your first day. Want to take a look?"

Sadie nodded, trying not to betray her shock. A potential murder case on her first day could be just what she needed to establish herself here and put the last case in DC behind her. But that wasn't the reason that her heart was thumping so loudly that she was amazed Golightly couldn't hear it.

A young woman, dumped in the frozen lakes on her first day back? Just like Jessica had been? Sadie wasn't given to superstition and knew as a BAU expert the importance of not seeing patterns that may not be there, but the eeriness of the coincidence wasn't lost on her.

Assuming it was a coincidence.

Sadie carefully arranged her face into a neutral but faintly eager expression, trying to strike the right balance between being ready to get stuck into her new job without betraying the fact that this case had already touched a very personal nerve.

"Although as you said, Sir, it is my first day. I wouldn't want to tread on anyone's toes," she said, although her whole body was itching to get out of her chair and investigate.

Golightly shrugged, clearly not too concerned with the digits of other officers. "You're the hotshot, Agent Price. Looks like you can start proving those credentials of yours straight away. You can start by getting yourself acquainted with the local Sheriff, although I'll warn you, he ain't usually too keen on our involvement."

"That's not uncommon; I can handle it," Sadie assured him. The ongoing antipathy between federal and state law enforcement bored her. As far as she was concerned, they were on the same side, and whoever the poor girl in the lake was, she deserved better than to have petty resentments stand in the way of justice. She wondered who the unidentified victim was.

"Good," Golightly said approvingly. "May as well get stuck in straight away. Not what you expected though, ay?"

"No, Sir." Sadie had been expecting to spend at least a few months dealing with nothing more harrowing than some mild drug dealing and firearms charges. Cases that were way below her level of experience, not to mention her pay grade, but that would have bought her time to reinvestigate her sister's death. There would be plenty of time for that, though. Right now, another young woman had her life cut short, and her body dumped in the lakes like so much rubbish. Sadie felt a surge of anger. Her exhaustion from the long drive and appetite for breakfast were forgotten. Getting settled into Anchorage could wait.

She leaned forward, feeling her detective instincts come to the fore.

"Any recent missing girls Sir? Or similar cases?"

Sadie felt a sudden sense of déjà vu. She fought against the memories that were fighting to resurface. Of another body, and another lake. Her sister's face surfaced in her mind, and she pushed the image away quickly.

She couldn't think about Jessica now. She blinked rapidly, forcing herself back into the present moment to listen to what the ASAC was telling her, letting her professional mindset take over. The rest could wait.

"Not that we're aware of Agent Price," Golightly said. "But given the time of year I bet the ME will find it almost impossible to tell when she was drowned, and there might not even be enough evidence to prove it a murder one way or the other. Ice preserves, but it destroys too. But you don't need me to tell me that, do you?"

Sadie flinched at his words, even though she knew he could only be referring to the fact that she was originally Alaskan. Golightly wasn't a local…he couldn't know about Jessica. Her death in the end had been written off as unexplained, and no one was ever questioned or charged. Sadie had never bought it.

She wasn't going to let the same thing happen again.

"Yes," Sadie agreed. "Which makes it the perfect medium for a murder." The hairs stood up on the back of her neck at her words and she knew that something was very off about this whole scenario.

"Let's not go jumping to any conclusions here Agent," Golightly said firmly, although the way he was drumming his fingers on his desk suggested that he was thinking along much the same lines. "Go and check it out and report back. Try not to tread on too many of those toes. Take O'Hara if you're not comfortable on your own...although it might be a bit much for the Sheriff."

"No, Sir, you're right, it will be better if I go alone," Sadie said, trying not to notice the disappointed look on O'Hara's face. "Best not to ruffle any local feathers on my first day."

"You're a local too," Golightly reminded her, "and if it does turn out to be something more sinister than an accident or domestic, then we're going to need you."

Sadie nodded and stood up, ready to go.

"Agent Price," Golightly said, calling her back.

"Yes, Sir?"

"Do not," he told her, looking grim, "let that damn Sheriff try and keep you away from the action."

CHAPTER THREE

Sadie followed O'Hara outside, where he gave her the address and the keys to the snow truck.

"You won't get up there otherwise," he told her. "Are you sure you'll be able to find it? It's a thirty-minute clear run, and then the last few miles will be off road."

Sadie nodded as she wrapped her scarf back around her face and pulled up her hood. "Sure," she replied as she climbed into the snowmobile, too quietly for Agent O'Hara to hear her through the fabric, "it's right next to my hometown."

Sadie drove off, the heavy wheels making deep tracks through the snow, and saw O'Hara wave at her in the rearview mirror. She almost wished she had brought him with her after all, if only to keep her mind focused and alert, instead of slipping back into the memories that she had once left Alaska in order to forget.

Her sister's face swam into her mind again, and again Sadie pushed it away.

Not now, she told herself firmly. Over the years, she had gotten pretty good at locking all those memories away, dormant until a time when she was ready to deal with them.

Focusing on the road ahead that led her out of Anchorage, she forced herself to think instead about the case at hand, wondering what she was about to find when she arrived at the scene, and just how unfriendly the Sheriff was likely to be. If Golightly's estimation of the man was correct, then he could be a real hindrance.

Talk about throwing her in at the deep end, on her first day.

As a federal agent, Sadie was used to dealing with antagonism from local cops; she understood it, even. It must be frustrating and even humiliating to be pushed aside on a case by the arrival of the FBI, especially if they had no local connection. She had known cops to take it personally when she showed up at a murder scene, and to even close ranks, making her job harder than it needed to be.

So, while she could understand their behavior, that didn't mean that she had to tolerate it. Sadie had no intention of letting Sheriff Cooper freeze her out of what could potentially be her first big case here, and her chance to impress Golightly.

It was odd, she mused, but she found herself wanting to impress the gruff old man. To prove that she was more than just an impressive resumé from Quantico and that she could cope with whatever Alaska had to throw at her. Although she thought the case in DC had tempered some of her ambition, she also felt something of her old drive coming back.

But this time, she told herself, she had to be careful.

In order to do that, however, she had to actually get to the crime scene. The road was clear enough until the built-up areas retreated. Then she found herself surrounded once again by swaths of snow and ice, punctuated only by the occasional cabin or forlorn looking shop.

The mid-morning light was dim, more like the evenings down south, and there were few other vehicles on the road. As she pulled up at a red-light, Sadie wondered what she was about to walk into, trying not to wince at a sudden intrusive thought of the young woman's frozen body. She had seen plenty of dead bodies in her career, but none that brought back echoes of her sister's death like this one did.

But she knew that she couldn't focus on that. Anchoring herself firmly in the present, she thought about the sparse information she had been given and wondered who the as yet unidentified victim was. A local, or a tourist, although they were rare this time of year.

The light changed to green, and she drove on, keeping her eyes on the snow-covered road until it ran out entirely and Sadie remembered why it took twice as long to get anywhere here. The snow truck was built for purpose and gamely took on the task at hand, churning up snow under its tracks, but her pace had slowed to a crawl, and it felt as though she was wrestling to get the truck over the ground. She peered through the window, realizing that everywhere now looked the same and wondering if she should have taken up O'Hara on his offer of directions.

The farther she got into the wilderness park, the harder it became to drive. The wind started to whip up and flurries of snow blew in front of her windscreen, obscuring her vision. It would be just her luck to get stuck in a snowbank on her first day.

As the lakes came into view, Sadie drew a breath, realizing the victim had been found very close to where her sister's body had been discovered all those years ago: the next lake along, in fact. Spotting the current crime scene was easy enough. Even before Sadie got close enough to make out the forensic tent and the vehicles of the Medical Examiner and the Sheriff himself, she saw the small crowd of onlookers, mostly other fishermen, keeping a less than respectable distance. Sadie sighed as she pulled the snow plough to a stop. The scene reminded her of the first murder in the Boston case, when the victim had been found in a local park and, like this one, attracted the morbid curiosity of passersby.

As she jumped down, she saw a woman in a cop's uniform striding towards her. With a ski-mask covering the woman's face, Sadie couldn't make out her expression, but the way her eyes bored into her indicated that Sadie's presence was less than unwelcome.

It looked as though it wouldn't just be Sheriff Cooper that she would have to deal with.

Sadie gave the woman a brisk nod as she approached. "I'm Special Agent Price," she said politely. "Anchorage Field Office have sent me over to assist you."

"We have plenty of assistance," the woman snapped with such hostility that Jane was taken aback. "There's no need for FBI involvement. This is an imposition."

Sadie felt herself bristle at the woman's tone, but her voice was cool as she replied.

"We were told the ME believes that she was forcibly drowned."

The woman rolled her eyes. "So, what, you guys want to make this into some big case? It will most likely turn out to be a domestic or drunken argument, if it turns out that she was drowned at all. Difficult to tell anything in these lakes. If you were from round here, you would know that. You're wasting your time; you can go back and tell Golightly that the Sheriff and myself have things under control."

Sadie raised an eyebrow. "Actually," she said in the same cool tone, determined not to let this person's hostility rattle her, "it's the Sheriff I need to speak to. Who are you, exactly?"

"Deputy Cooper." The deputy practically spit out her words.

"Oh? Any relation?"

"The Sheriff is my brother, not that it has any relevance to anything."

Great, Jane thought, *I have two of them to deal with.*

"Perhaps you could take me to him?" Sadie suggested. Deputy Cooper looked like that was the last thing she wanted to do but seemed to finally realize that she had little choice as she turned and walked back towards the lake, Sadie following.

They walked through the small crowd of onlookers and Sadie saw the heads craning to watch her, regarding her with morbid curiosity. She kept her eyes on the tent ahead, hoping that she wasn't about to hear someone say her name in recognition. Someone who had once known her, or worse, still knew her father. His cabin was just a few miles from the main fishing lakes.

Sadie had no intention of visiting.

Once they were past the police tape, she caught up with the Deputy. "The man who found her," she said, "what's the deal with him? Has he been ruled out as a suspect?"

The policewoman glared at her. "Obviously," she said, her voice dripping with sarcasm, "he has been thoroughly questioned."

"And?" Sadie pressed. Deputy Cooper stopped walking and shook her head in exasperation.

"Are you questioning our ability to do our jobs? "

"No," Sadie said patiently, although she was feeling anything but. She hadn't even met the Sherriff or seen the body yet, and this woman was seriously getting on her nerves. "But I will have to report back to the ASAC, and so it's important that I have all the details. Unless you want me to report back that I'm unable to do so because you refused to cooperate?"

Deputy Cooper looked furious, but also knew that she ultimately had no choice but to answer Sadie's questions. Ignoring Sadie's threat, she said sullenly, "Mr. Willoughby has been sent home after being checked over for shock. We will question him again if we need to, but right now there is no reason not to believe his story. He reeled her in a few hours ago, during his usual early morning fishing. His wife corroborated that he usually goes out at that time."

"Could give him the perfect cover story," Sadie commented, although she knew she was baiting the Deputy more than anything else. It made little sense that Willoughby would reel the body back in rather than leaving it under the ice, where it could go undiscovered for years, if not forever. Particularly with no missing report. "We still don't know who she is?"

"No," the Deputy said shortly, "*We* don't." Her emphasis made it quite clear that Sadie wasn't included. Sadie ignored her and headed towards the pop-up forensics unit, leaving the Deputy to now follow her.

As she entered the tent, both the Medical Examiner and the Sheriff looked up and nodded at her. The ME looked friendly enough, but she saw that Sheriff Cooper's eyes glimmered with the same suspicion as his sister's, although he didn't appear quite so obviously hostile, which was a relief. Dealing with them both could quickly become a real ball ache.

"This is Special Agent Price, come all the way from the Field Office to help out us poor hicks," the Deputy said behind her, voice dripping with sarcasm. Once again Sadie swallowed her anger at the woman's attitude. There were more important things to think about now.

Like the victim, lying frozen in front of her.

She avoided looking at the unfortunate girl's body as she held a hand out to Sheriff Cooper and introduced herself. He took it reluctantly, dropping it as soon as he could.

"I don't think that this warrants Federal involvement, not at this stage," he said, echoing his sister. He was tall, Sadie noted, with broad shoulders, dark hair and eyes that were startlingly green against olive skin. He could be handsome, she thought, if only his expression wasn't so sour.

"Hopefully, that will be the case," Sadie said, her voice deliberately neutral. "If you and your Deputy here can let me do my job, we can find that out, can't we?"

The Sheriff's eyes flickered over her shoulder towards his sister, then back to Sadie, who thought that she saw a glimpse of grudging respect in them. That was a start.

Finally, she turned towards the ME. Towards the body.

Keeping her face very carefully composed, refusing to let either of the siblings see that she felt any discomfort, Sadie's eyes swept the corpse of the young woman that had been hauled in from the lake that morning. As expected, her body was blue and bloated, her features engorged no doubt beyond recognition. Sadie wondered how long she had been there, trapped under the icy surface, and tried not to think about her sister. She couldn't afford to let the grief in, not here.

Or the guilt.

"Do we have any update on an ID?" she said instead. The ME answered her. He was an older man, tall and slender with detached gray eyes. He shook his head.

"Not as of yet. The fact that it's almost impossible to pinpoint a time of death doesn't help, as she could have been under the ice for months, even longer. It really doesn't give us much to go on. There are some marks around her neck there that indicate forced drowning, but her body is so discolored it's impossible to be sure. Or to prove."

Sadie glanced at the girl's face. Her lips were curled back in what looked like a grimace of fear, and she wondered what her final moments had been like. Had she seen her attacker's face? Did she know them? Sadie somehow knew instinctively that they were looking at a murder, and a brutal one at that. She felt a wave of compassion for the unknown girl, hoping that her end had been quick.

"Any signs of molestation? Missing digits or hair – signs that a trophy has been taken?"

The ME shook his head as the Sheriff cut in, sounding annoyed.

"I know you guys like to jump to conclusions, but let's try not to get ahead of ourselves, hey?"

Sadie gave him a polite, fixed smile, stopping herself from biting back in kind. She had no time for this. If there was someone out there hiding the bodies of young women in the lakes, then they needed to be caught as soon as possible.

Because for all they knew, this might not be the only body out there. There were dozens of these lakes, connected by the underground currents, and they all held their own secrets.

"Any missing persons reports? Any young women recently left town with a boyfriend, gone off to college, anything like that?"

"Obviously that was the first thing we checked," the Sheriff said shortly. "We've put a report out on the morning news. No. We have no idea who she is so far. Like the Doc here says, she could have been here for months. We just have to hope that the prints and dental records will turn something up."

Sadie's eyes swept the body again as she swallowed the empathy that naturally arose for the girl's tragic fate, and instead appraised her with the professional logic that she had been taught to use. She doubted that there would be anything to find, as there was no reason to think that the ME had missed anything, but experience had taught her to double and triple check everything. No one was infallible. Details could be missed, and those details could be crucial.

Something about the corpse's hands caught her attention, and Sadie leaned down to look closer. Even with the metallic blue tinge on her grossly swollen fingers, Sadie was sure that she could see tell-tale signs that would indicate a much more recent time of death. Signs the ME would not necessarily recognize.

“There. There are small burns on her fingers,” she said quietly. The ME followed her gaze, peering at the dead girl’s hands.

“Possibly…as I said, there is so much discoloration it would be hard to tell.” He looked over the body and frowned. “Hmmm…that mark on her lips looks the same.”

Sadie nodded, knowing now that her hunch was right. In the city, she had seen this too many times to be mistaken.

“Burns. From the ice?” the Sheriff said incredulously. Sadie straightened up and looked him square in the face.

“She was a meth user, Sheriff,” she told him, “The pattern and location of those marks are consistent with use of a meth pipe. And those burns will be recent. A few days at most.”

She saw the surprise and then the grudging respect dawn in the Sheriff’s eyes as he nodded, absorbing the information. The ME swore under his breath.

“I should have spotted that,” he said, sounding angry at himself. “It explains her teeth too; they are quite decayed.”

“Yes. We call it ‘meth mouth.’ She must have been a hardcore user; and that means she had a dealer,” Sadie went on. “Who might well have been one of the last people to see her and would be able to ID her.”

She saw the Sheriff glance at his sister over her shoulder.

“Do you know any local meth dealers?” she pressed. The Sheriff nodded.

“Yes. I can take you to him now.”

“Good,” Sadie said. “Let’s go.”

CHAPTER FOUR

Sadie glanced across at Sheriff Cooper, wondering where he was going. He had seemed to be heading back towards town, only to veer away just before the sign for Anchorage and head in the direction of the pine-covered mountains. She was about to mention the fact that the way she remembered it, the only people who lived out this way were the fishermen and hunters; then at the last minute she remembered that Sheriff Cooper didn't know that she was a local.

It shouldn't matter, Sadie told herself. Her past was her business and had nothing to do with either the Sheriff or his hostile sibling, yet for some reason she felt wary of telling him too much about herself. He was already resentful of her involvement, and she sensed that if he knew she wasn't entirely an outsider it would only make his resentment worse.

She also didn't want to feel judged. The questions about why she had left would come eventually; Sadie knew that she couldn't avoid them forever. But she didn't feel up to answering them just yet.

Especially now, with this first case dragging up too many painful memories. Bringing them up into the light just as the lakes had given up the bodies of the victims.

As though reading her mind, Cooper's voice broke the silence between them. "That was good work, spotting those marks on her fingers, especially when the rest of us missed them."

The praise was grudging, but it was there, and Sadie felt oddly pleased that her first impression hadn't been all bad.

"Thanks."

Cooper suddenly seemed to want to make conversation.

"It isn't the first thing you tend to look for, around here. We don't get a lot of drug related killings. That's usually all guns and gangs, isn't it?

Sadie didn't respond, guessing that Cooper wouldn't be impressed by a rundown of her knowledge of gang killers.

"I suppose you saw this kind of thing a lot back in DC. Drugs, I mean."

"Some." Sadie glanced at him sideways, trying to read him. "Things tend to get nasty when drugs are involved. Does Anchorage have much of a meth problem?" She bit back the 'these days' that would have followed on the end of her question. She didn't remember meth being much of a thing back when she was growing up here. Instead, there were nights by the lakes, with stolen bottles of vodka from someone's parents' drinks cupboard.

Times had changed.

Cooper nodded; his full mouth scrunched up in disapproval.

"In the last few years, it seems to have spread like wildfire. You always get the odd few, of course, but it's growing now. There's too little for people to do here, and jobs are scarce these days. There hasn't been much related violence though, other than a few domestics."

Sadie didn't remember it ever being any different in that regard.

"So, the dealer we're going to see," she said, "Tell me about him?"

"His name is Peter Montgomery," Cooper said, and his expression soured even more. "Fancies himself as our local drugs kingpin and seems to be something of a part-time pimp too. Total lowlife."

Sadie raised her eyebrows at the name. There had been a Peter Montgomery a few years above her at school, and from what she remembered of him, ending up as a meth dealer wasn't too much of a shock. It had to be the same guy.

If Montgomery remembered her too, then the Sheriff was going to find out her history sooner than she would have liked. Still, she sighed to herself, it was going to come out sooner or later. She couldn't avoid it forever.

"Does he have any previous?" she asked.

The Sheriff nodded. "Possession, mostly, but never enough to put him away for a decent amount of time. He's cleverer than he looks."

Sadie was about to mention the fact that she suspected she might know him when Cooper pulled up in front of a large and decrepit country house. The ground floor shutters were hanging off and tiles were visibly missing from the roof. It had certainly seen better days. She vaguely remembered Peter bragging about his granddaddy living in a big house and guessed that the old man had left it to his grandson. Probably not with the intention of it being used as a meth den and brothel.

The snow crunched under foot as they approached the front door, announcing their arrival. It seemed to be picking up as the day progressed. Cooper knocked, calling Montgomery's name as he did so.

Sadie took a deep breath, hoping that the man wouldn't remember her. School was a long time ago, and they hadn't exactly been friends.

The door was snatched open and a tall, scruffy looking man with greasy hair tied back in a ponytail stood there, glaring at Cooper. His dark eyes were bloodshot, and he needed a shave. The smell of marijuana clung to him. "What do you want?" he snapped. "Harassing me again, are you?"

"We just need to ask a few questions, Peter, nothing to worry about," Cooper said smoothly. He gestured to Sadie. "This is Special Agent Price."

A look of fear flashed over Montgomery's face. "The feds? What's this all about, man? You said nothing to worry about!" He turned to Sadie, looking her up and down, and she swallowed her disappointment as she saw the recognition dawn in his eyes.

"Sadie? Little Sadie from school? You're a Fed? What the hell!" He laughed, as though he had never heard anything so funny in his life. With a tight smile, Sadie flashed him her badge.

"That's right, Peter. I'm a Fed. So, do you think we could come in? It's pretty cold out here."

Montgomery stopped laughing. For a moment he looked as though he might refuse, but then he reluctantly grunted his assent and stepped aside to let them in. Sadie went in, deliberately avoiding looking at Cooper, whose eyes she could feel boring into her as she passed him.

The inside of the house was as dilapidated as its exterior, and Montgomery led them through to a large kitchen with a sink piled up with dishes, bags of rubbish on the floor and stains up the wall that Sadie decided she didn't even want to think about. If he had become the local drugs baron, he clearly wasn't spending his profits on décor. Or a housekeeper.

"I didn't think we would see you around here again," Montgomery said to Sadie. There was a slight sneer to his voice, which fit with her recollections of him. He had been a few years older than her in school and so not part of her immediate social circle, but she had known who he was. They all did. He was a bully, but also a reliable source, for those who wanted them, of both marijuana and alcohol, as well as harder substances.

Some things obviously hadn't changed.

"Perhaps we could leave the high school reunion until later?" Cooper said drily. He wasn't looking at Sadie, but she could sense the anger underneath his words and guessed that he was annoyed with her for not telling him.

They could deal with that later. Right now, they needed to identify the victim. She looked at Peter Montgomery, wondering if the boy she remembered could have turned into a murderer as well as a drug dealer and pimp. It wasn't so much of a leap, in her experience, but as Cooper had said, this was hardly gang territory. If anything, Montgomery's set up was likely to be something of a cottage industry, with few if any rivals.

"I need to show you some pictures," Cooper said, taking a few of the crime scene photos from his inside pocket. "Be warned, they are not pretty. We found a body in the lakes this morning."

"Body?" Montgomery said with what looked to be genuine surprise. "What's that got to do with me? I ain't killed anyone."

"We didn't say anyone had been killed," Sadie challenged.

"You wouldn't be here otherwise," he said and folded his arms mutinously.

"Just look at the picture, Peter," Sadie said softly, and was surprised when he did as she asked.

Cooper showed the man the first photograph and Sadie saw his beady eyes widen with recognition. "Yeah," he said, looking visibly shaken even though his tone aimed for nonchalance. "Yeah, I know her. Her name's Verity Hagen."

"How do you know her?" Sadie cut in.

Montgomery hesitated and then shrugged. "She used to work for me, but not anymore. She got a new boyfriend about two months ago and I haven't heard from her since."

"You're not dealing to her?" Cooper was blunt.

Montgomery shuffled uncomfortably. "Don't know what you mean, man."

Cooper gave a sigh and Sadie decided this was her cue to step in. She stepped forward, smiling at Montgomery.

"Peter," she said, her voice formal but friendly, her continued use of his first name reminding him of their scrap of shared history, "we're not here to ask you about your…business enterprises. We need to work out what happened to Verity. Who might have seen her last, and how she ended up in the lake. We know that she used recently, so if she wasn't getting her gear from you, then who?"

Montgomery shook his head. "Sorry Sadie, I can't help you." Again, she caught a note of fear in his voice and knew instinctively that he knew more than he was letting on. She was about to speak when Cooper cut in.

"I don't have time to play games, Montgomery. You need to tell us what you know. Or I might decide I am interested in your little 'enterprise,' after all."

Montgomery folded his arms and glared at the Sheriff. "Go ahead," he challenged. "You won't find anything in here. Besides, you don't have a warrant. I told you, this is police harassment."

"No one is harassing you, Peter," Sadie said in a soothing voice, wishing that Cooper would take the hint and keep quiet. His strong-arm tactics were just going to aggravate Montgomery, and he would tell them nothing. "But we do need to know any information that you happen to have on Verity. You said she worked for you?"

Montgomery nodded, having enough decency to look slightly shamefaced. "Yeah, she was an escort. I just help, you know, manage the bookings. For dates, that's all. Nothing to do with me what goes on when she gets there." He was defensive, and with good reason; sentences for facilitating prostitution could be harsh. Rightly so, in Sadie's opinion. There were few things as morally repugnant in her eyes as a man making money from the bodies of vulnerable women, who were, in her experience, most likely to be underage, fresh out of the care system or on drugs. Quite often, all three at once.

She nodded carefully, trying not to show her distaste. As much as she wanted to arrest Montgomery there and then, his prostitution racket wasn't why they were there.

She felt sure now that Verity's death had been no accident. The girl was, if the ID was correct, both a heavy drug user and a hooker. The statistics on meeting a non-violent death or living a long life were not in her favor.

"Like Sheriff Cooper said, we're not here for you, Peter."

"Not yet," Cooper snapped. Sadie ignored him.

"We just need to get an idea of what was going on for Verity in the last days of her life. People will be missing her."

Montgomery sneered, as though he couldn't imagine why anyone would miss her, and Sadie had to swallow her sudden anger at his attitude. Whatever Verity Hagen had done or been, she was also a human being, a young woman who still might have had time to turn her life around. She should never have ended up floating under the lakes with the only person to identify her being her former pimp.

"Alright; I let her go. Her habit was getting out of control. Last I heard, she had hooked up with a mutual friend, someone else you might remember from school."

Sadie felt her stomach sink. Her first case was turning out to be all too close to home. First, the painful similarities to her sister's death, and now this.

"Go on," she prompted, ignoring the feeling of nausea.

"Matthew Collins." Montgomery smirked as her as Sadie blinked in surprise.

Matthew had been her boyfriend in high school. It had been puppy love, nothing more, but her memories of him were fond enough. The class clown, with a shock of bright blond hair and a charming smile, he was the last person she would have expected to grow up and be involved in something like this. She tried to hide her shock as she looked sideways at Cooper. "Do you know him?"

"Not offhand," Cooper replied, not looking at her. She felt relieved that at least Matthew hadn't picked up a record. "Was he a user too?" she asked Montgomery, who nodded.

"Yeah, a heavy one. Always getting into debt, and not just to me. He borrows money anywhere he can, when he's not stealing it. Total loser. Like I said, the last I heard Verity was shacked up with him and he was pimping her out to all comers. It must have gone south. Both a pair of deadbeats."

"As opposed to you, of course. You seem to have done really well for yourself, Peter," Sadie said coolly, no longer bothering to hide her opinion of the man in front of her. He glared at her.

"You always did think you were too good for the rest of us, Price," he spat, and she saw the viciousness in his eyes. He could play dumb all he liked, but Sadie had no doubt that he was capable of killing Verity Hague, even if he wasn't actually guilty of the act. So far, there was no reason to rule him out – but no reason to bring him in, either.

"That's enough," Cooper warned.

"Yeah, it is enough," Montgomery glowered. "Unless you have a lawyer, I ain't answering anymore of your questions."

"If we have any, I'll let you know," Cooper said. "We can see ourselves out." He left and Sadie followed, being careful not to brush up against the walls.

"See you soon, Sadie!" Montgomery called after her in a mocking voice.

Sadie got back into Cooper's truck as he radioed the Deputy and got a current address for Matthew Collins. He got in beside her, barely glancing at her, and Sadie wondered when, not if, the questions would come. She couldn't avoid them forever.

"Right," he said instead, revving the engine, "Let's pay a visit to your other school friend, shall we?"

CHAPTER FIVE

Sadie felt tiredness threaten to overwhelm her as they drove, and she blinked rapidly against it. The snow had picked up again, along with the wind. The dancing snowflakes in front of the truck, a flurry of white against an even whiter background, were almost hypnotic in their movement.

It had been hours since she had gotten any sleep, and she hadn't eaten since yesterday evening. It was approaching mid-morning and Sadie's stomach grumbled audibly, making her wince in embarrassment.

Cooper didn't seem to notice. He had other things on his mind.

"At any point," he said in a deliberately measured tone that belied the angry set of his jaw, "were you going to mention that you were a local?"

Sadie shrugged, too tired to get into it. Her focus now was on finding out as much as she could about poor Verity Hagen, before the need for sleep forced her off the job for the day. "Is it relevant, Sheriff?"

"I would say so, seeing as you seem to know all of our suspects so far."

"Are they suspects? That seems a little premature." She was sniping, she knew, echoing his own words earlier when she had speculated about what had befallen Verity. With her stomach grumbling and her nerves frayed, she was past caring.

Cooper took his eyes off the road to glare at her. "You should have told me. It's bad enough having a Fed come in and take over…" he bit off his words, perhaps realizing that he had said more than he wanted to, and Sadie felt a pang of sympathy for him in spite of her irritation.

She tried to look at things from his point of view. The fact that she was a local, rather than endearing her to him, might make him feel even more threatened. He couldn't simply dismiss her as some hotshot Fed with big ideas who didn't know a thing about the area, when it seemed she knew the potential suspects better than he did.

Taking a deep breath, she decided to tell him about her school romance with Matthew. Although she was never comfortable giving out personal information, Sadie knew that if she was to hold back on any more details then Cooper would take it personally. He already didn't trust her.

She opened her mouth to both apologize and tell him about Matthew, but Cooper spoke over her, cutting her off before she could finish her first word.

"You made me look stupid in there," he continued. "I should have known. This is always how you guys operate though isn't it, holding things back from us?"

"I don't think Montgomery noticed," Sadie said, deciding that Cooper could stick any apology. This was her life he was talking about, not some silly feud between the local cops and the Feds. "This isn't personal, Cooper," she said shortly. "I only arrived in town this morning, right before the call came in. I came straight out to the crime scene, where I can't say either you or your sister were particularly welcoming, and then we came out to Montgomery. There hasn't exactly been time for us to have a heart to heart about my background. And quite frankly, at this juncture it's none of your damn business."

It dawned on her that she had fought at the precinct to not have a partner but now she had one in Sheriff Cooper anyway. Perhaps she should have let O'Hara come along after all.

Cooper pulled a face at her retort but didn't reply. They drove on in an increasingly loaded silence, the tension between them palpable.

Sadie looked out of the window as the outskirts of the town came into view through the snow, wondering where Matthew Collins lived now. When they were kids, his parents had a convenience shop up by the lakes, not far from where Verity had been found, running a successful store full of hunting and fishing gear, the favorite of the seasonal tourists. Not that she had given much, if any, thought to Matthew over the years, but she would have expected him to have taken over the family store.

Instead, Cooper had turned off the main road and was heading towards the poorest part of town, where the houses became increasingly more rundown. Some of them would make Montgomery's place look like a celebrity mansion. They passed a battered looking saloon bar that still had a flickering neon sign in spite of its boarded-up windows, and then Cooper pulled up in front of a ramshackle little cabin that looked in serious danger of falling down.

"This is where Collins lives?"

"Yep," Cooper said grimly. "Not what you imagined?"

Sadie shook her head as she wrapped her scarf around her face before getting out of the truck.

"It doesn't fit with what I remember of him. Do his parents still run the store up at the lakes?"

Cooper nodded but didn't elaborate. Sadie wondered what Matthew's parents thought of their son's apparent decline into meth addiction. Whether they were supportive, or if they had cut their son off, unable to watch the descent.

It happened up here; she knew that all too well. The loneliness and lack of employment could get too much for anyone, and while she didn't remember meth being common, Anchorage had always had its fair share of junkies and drunks, just like any city and town in America.

Just like her father. He had always been a drinker, but after her mother and then sister's death it had gotten steadily worse, until drink had eclipsed whatever personality he might have had. Not that Sadie remembered him ever being particularly loving towards her. A doting dad, he certainly hadn't been.

"Ready?" Cooper peered at her and she snapped out of her reverie.

"Sorry, yes, of course."

"If you want to sit this one out…conflict of interest and all that…," Cooper said, sarcasm dripping from his voice. Sadie shot him a look.

"I'm fine, Sheriff. The fact that I know Collins might well be an advantage." She stormed ahead of him to knock on the door, annoyed with herself for getting distracted and letting Cooper see it.

The man that opened the door looked so unlike the boy that Sadie remembered that she at first assumed he wasn't Matthew. His head was shaved, his clothes hung from his skinny frame, and his pupils were so dilated that his eyes were almost black in his gaunt face, which was pocked with telltale scabs, especially around his mouth. He looked like the 'Before' picture in an advert for drug rehabilitation.

Then he looked at Sadie and his eyes widened in recognition.

"Sadie Price? What are you doing here?" He sounded overjoyed to see her and she almost felt sorry for him. Especially when she flashed her badge and saw the shock on his face, as he realized that this was no impromptu school reunion.

Then she remembered that he might be the last person to ever see Verity Hagen alive. Assuming that he wasn't responsible, she wondered if he was even aware of the girl's death.

“We need to ask you a few questions, Matthew. Can we come inside?”

Matthew hesitated, looking over her shoulder at Cooper, then his whole body seemed to deflate as he stood aside and let them in.

Sadie knew what to expect, but even so, the interior made her stomach roll, and she was almost glad it was empty. The small house was filthy and smelled of mold and dirty bodies. As Matthew showed them into what passed for a lounge, Sadie wasn’t surprised to see that there was no furniture other than a ripped up old sofa and a small coffee table littered with drug paraphernalia, although no actual meth was on show. Matthew would have stashed that before answering the door.

“That isn’t mine,” he said weakly, gesturing at the table. He seemed defeated, with no real fight in him. What had happened to him? Sadie felt a rush of anger at Montgomery and those like him, who preyed on people weaker than themselves, before reminding herself not to let her heart rule her head. Matthew wasn’t the boy she remembered, and this might well all be an act. Being soft-hearted was a hindrance in her job, not a help.

She had made that mistake before, and she had no intention of ever doing so again.

“It’s so good to see you though, Sadie,” Matthew said before she or Cooper could reply. There was something of the kid that she remembered in his smile, and she recalled a memory of walking through the parks with him as a teenager in the summer, hand in hand, secure in the knowledge that they had their entire lives in front of them. After her sister had died Matthew had been kind to her; in fact, he had been the only person who had truly been there for her. She had never expected to see him like this, and she couldn’t help but feel a small lingering of affection for him, or at least for the version of him that she had known.

“You too, Matthew,” she said briskly, swallowing all of the questions she had about the years she had been gone, and how the hell he had ended up here. “Unfortunately, we’re here about Verity. She was found drowned this morning.”

Matthew slumped and his eyes went to the ground. She watched him carefully for signs of guilt.

“I heard that a body was found in the lakes. They were talking about it in the saloon this morning. I just knew it would be her; she’s been missing for a few days. I didn't think anything of it at first, she does her own thing, but then when I heard that, I just knew."

"This morning?" Sadie raised an eyebrow. It was barely noon.

"Yeah. Caz – that's the owner – opens up early sometimes. Some of the fishermen come down, especially if they've had a bad catch. Drown their sorrows and all that."

Sadie wanted to ask if he ever saw her father in there, but this wasn't the time, especially in front of Cooper. She doubted her dad was any less of a recluse than before, which suited her just fine. Her father was the last person that she needed to be bumping into in the course of her inquiries. She wondered how long it would be before he heard that she was back. If he would care.

"When did you last see her, Matthew? We were told Verity was your girlfriend, is that right?"

Matthew's right eye flickered, a tic that Sadie suddenly remembered. He was about to lie to them, or at the very least to be evasive with the truth.

"No! She was…just a friend. That's all. A friend."

"We heard you were pimping her out," Cooper cut in harshly and for the first time Matthew looked angry, his mouth curling into an expression that could only be described as a snarl. With his dilated eyes he looked feral.

There were flecks of white at the corner of his mouth and Sadie suppressed a shudder of revulsion. Matthew was strung out and it showed. It was such a sudden change in his composure, and she realized that he was a stranger to her now. The Matthew that she had once held hands with and had her first kiss with by the lakes had been consumed by his addiction.

"You heard that from who?" Matthew retorted. "Peter? He's the pimp, not me. He got Verity hooked and then pimped her out and paid her in meth. It's what he does to all of his girls. She was a mess; I tried to help her, that's all."

"Bu using drugs with her? Very charitable of you," Cooper said. Matthew looked for a second as though he would spring at the Sheriff, but then he sagged again, looking at Sadie with pleading eyes.

"So, you weren't having any kind of sexual relationship with her, Matthew?" Sadie said, not giving him an inch. He was hiding something, and she wanted to know what it was. Matthew sighed heavily and sat down with a soft thump on the broken armchair.

"She wasn't my girlfriend," he repeated. His hands were twitching. From fear or because he needed another hit? Sadie was prepared to bet that it would be a combination of both. "It wasn't like us. You were my first love Sadie; did you know that?"

Sadie felt her cheeks burn as Cooper's head whipped round, his nostrils flaring as he looked at Sadie. This was the second time she had withheld information from him in his eyes, and Sadie knew that this was going to seriously piss him off. Perhaps she should have mentioned it on the drive over after all, even if he had been a dick.

"But you had some kind of relationship with her?" she pressed, ignoring Matthew's comment. Matthew nodded.

"Yeah, I guess. She was a hooker. I hired her a few times, then we became friends. I felt sorry for her. Peter is a bastard; she needed to get away from him."

"So, you helped her get away?"

Matthew shrugged. "Not really. Peter was pretty much done with her; she was all used up he said. It's what he does," he repeated, sounding disgusted. The irony wasn't lost on Sadie or the Sheriff, who made a scoffing noise in the back of his throat.

"You look well, Sadie," Matthew said, changing the subject abruptly. He looked her up and down, and the appreciation in his eyes made her skin crawl. "I'm glad to see you've done good for yourself. Dunno why you would come back though. Especially after everything."

Out of the corner of her eyes Sadie saw Cooper glance at her again, this time with curiosity. "Thanks, but this isn't a social call," she said quickly, cutting him off before he could mention her sister. The similarities between Jessica's death and Verity's couldn't be lost on Matthew, either. "We need the truth, Matthew. Did you pimp her out, or not?"

Matthew hesitated, and Sadie already knew the answer before he gave it. "Not pimping, exactly," he said, avoiding her eyes. "Like I said, I helped her out."

Sadie felt any lingering affection for him vanish at his confession. Keeping her voice carefully neutral to hide her disgust, she said evenly, "What kind of help?"

Matthew shuffled uncomfortably, tapping his thigh urgently as though he had lost control of his fingers. He must be desperate for a hit.

"I drove her around. Let her bring a couple of johns back here."

"And took part of the money in return?"

Matthew shrugged. "She offered. For rent and stuff. I wasn't pimping her," he said again, but Sadie knew it was more to avoid arrest than because he believed his actions were in any way charitable. She looked at Cooper, hoping that if nothing else he would bring Matthew in for facilitating prostitution. Verity had clearly been vulnerable, and Matthew had only exploited her further, in order to feed his own habit. Sadie had seen it too many times before to feel anything but contempt for him now, regardless of their past relationship. She felt sick at the thought that he had once been her boyfriend.

"Any trouble with any of the johns?" Cooper asked. "Any violence, or just a general bad vibe? Stalking, odd comments, that sort of thing?"

Matthew shook his head. "Not that she told me about. She didn't talk about it much."

Sadie wondered if he would have cared.

"When was the last time you saw Verity?" she asked him.

"Dunno…a few days ago? She went off to score and didn't come back. Like I said, I wasn't worried at first. I'm not her keeper."

"Who did she score off?" Cooper cut in. "Still Peter, or someone else?"

Matthew smirked. "I'm not gonna tell you that," he said. "You think I'm some kind of grass?"

Cooper rolled his eyes. "Right now, I'm not interested in who is or isn't cooking up meth. I want to know how Verity ended up in that lake."

Matthew stopped smirking. "You don't think it was an accident, do you?" His eyes flickered to Sadie, taking in the badge on her coat, and she saw realization dawn in his eyes. He stood up, his right leg now twitching uncontrollably.

"Are you arresting me?"

"We're just asking a few questions," Cooper said smoothly. "No need to get excited."

"Do you know why Verity might have been at the lakes, Matthew?" Sadie asked. Matthew shook his head, but she saw sure that she saw that telltale flicker in his eye again.

"I want you to go," he said, his eyes darting around the room wildly.

"I just have a few more questions, Matthew. Nothing to worry about," Sadie said, trying to reassure him. The last thing they needed was a paranoid meth head on their hands and judging by the way he was now looking at them, he was getting more paranoid by the minute.

"What questions?" Matthew's voice was loud, and he was practically bouncing on the soles of his feet, his eyes wild. The atmosphere in the room was suddenly charged, and Sadie noticed Cooper subtly change position, his whole body tensing as though he was ready for an attack. She looked at Matthew and thought that in this mood, he might well be capable of murder. Perhaps he and Verity had argued, or she had failed to earn enough to keep them in meth? A chill went through her at the thought of the gentle boy that she had once been fond of becoming a killer.

Just then, Cooper's phone rang shrilly. The noise startled Matthew, making him visibly jump. The anger seemed to drain out of him, and he looked as though he was about to cry. Grief, or perhaps guilt, Sadie wondered? Or, just as likely, he was concerned he was going to end up in an Anchorage jail cell with no way to get the substances he so badly needed.

Cooper stepped to the side of the room to answer his cell, speaking in grunts. When he ended the call, he had a look of something in his eyes that Sadie recognized excitement.

They had a lead of some kind.

"Who was that?" Matthew demanded, sounding panicked as his paranoia grew again. He backed away across the room, eyeing Cooper's phone as though it was about to attack him.

"Nothing that you need to worry about, Matthew," the Sheriff said. He eyed the other man's appearance and Sadie saw him subtly shift his body language, his hand resting on the top of his thigh near to his holster. Preparing himself in case Matthew suddenly went on the attack. The long shirt Matthew was wearing cold easily conceal a gun or a knife, and a tweaker with a weapon was never fun to be around.

"I want you to go," he repeated, his eyes swiveling to look at Sadie. She saw the pleading in them, and she smiled the way one would at an anxious but feral dog.

"We won't keep you too long," Sadie assured him again. "But you may have been the last person to see Verity, and anything you know, even if it doesn't seem relevant right now, could be crucial to our investigation."

"I already told you, I don't know anything," he protested. "I don't know why she would be at the lakes; she never went there before."

"Could she have been meeting someone, one of the ice fishermen perhaps?" Cooper cut in. "Those guys can get pretty lonely when they're single."

"I don't know anything about her tricks," Matthew said stubbornly. The Sheriff noticeably rolled his eyes.

"Come on, you just told us you let Verity bring a couple of johns back here. Who were they?"

"I don't know," the man insisted. "I left them to it, I wasn't exactly up for making friends. Just a couple guys from the other side of town. They were regulars, she said. They didn't make any trouble."

"Did you get their first names?" Sadie pressed. Matthew shook his head, his left eye twitching furiously, and Sadie could see that they weren't going to get any more out of him that morning. It would be better to come back when he wasn't clearly withdrawing and desperate for a hit. Anything he told them in this state was likely to be unreliable in any case. Still, she wanted to know who Verity's local 'clients' had been. The statistics were clear for the murders of sex workers; if it wasn't a pimp, the next favorite was a punter.

"No, why would I? I didn't care who they were. Neither did Verity; they were a paycheck, that's all."

"One that you were happy to help her spend," Cooper said drily, his expression not even attempting to hide his disgust. He looked over at Sadie and an unspoken agreement passed between them. It was time to leave. They were getting nothing out of Matthew Collins that morning, and Sadie wanted to know what that phone call had been about.

"Stay out of trouble Matthew; we may still have more questions for you," the Sheriff said to the twitching young man in front of them. Matthew didn't answer or move to see them out, but just stared at them as they left, his shoulders visibly sagging with relief.

Sadie followed Cooper outside without looking at her high school boyfriend. It was painful to see him like this, but she also couldn't let any misplaced sympathy cloud her judgment.

She could be looking at a killer.

Outside, Sadie turned to the Sheriff. "Was the call about the case?" she asked, eager to know more.

"We're going to pay a visit to the saloon," Cooper said, his forehead creased.

"The saloon?" Sadie said, puzzled. What were they going to do, break up a bar fight? She shook her head in disappointment as she followed him to his vehicle.

"I'm wondering if we need to bring Matthew in," she said as she strapped herself into the passenger seat. "Although he's not likely to be much use to us at the minute. But you saw the way he was behaving; he could easily have killed Verity while he was high or tweaking. He's unstable, and that could make him dangerous."

"I don't think it's him," the Sheriff said. "I think asking about the johns was the better angle."

"There's a high statistical likelihood that one of them is the killer," Sadie agreed, "but Matthew was living with Verity and using with her. Things could easily have ended up in a fight."

"We will speak to him again, but right now we're going to the saloon," Cooper said again, and this time there was something in his tone that stopped Sadie in her tracks.

Whatever the call was about, this was no bar fight.

"What is it?" she asked, frowning.

"We might just need you after all," Cooper said, his voice grim. "Seems our killer might have sent us a little message."

CHAPTER SIX

The interior of the saloon had a musty smell to it that made Sadie wrinkle her nose as she walked in. It was dark, with only one intermittent lightbulb half-heartedly illuminating the room. A moose's head adorned the wall behind the bar, an outraged expression on its face as though horrified it was fated to spend its stuffed afterlife here rather than a more upmarket hunter's lodge. Sadie could feel it's pain.

At this time of day, the place was quiet but far from empty. A table of men playing cards swiveled their heads to look at Sadie and the Sherriff as they walked in, swiveling quickly back around when they saw their badges.

A few lone men and one woman nursed half empty glasses at solitary tables, and a group of three younger men stood at the bar, muttering between themselves as they watched them enter. Sadie felt her stomach tighten as she recognized two of them; one, the eldest of the two, was an old acquaintance of her father's, and the other she vaguely remembered from school. He had been in Peter's year although not, as far as Sadie could recall, a friend.

Ignoring the eyes that were peering at her, Sadie followed Cooper to the bar, where a heavyset and heavily tattooed woman with short red hair watched them approach.

"Caz," Cooper said in greeting. His voice seemed to soften as he spoke to her, and Sadie figured they were friends. Either that or she was just already used to him sounding pissed off. At least whatever this was about had distracted him from Sadie and Matthew's past for a while.

"Logan," the woman replied. "Sorry to call you out like this, but I've received something that you might want to get a look at, given the bad news this morning."

"What time did it arrive?" Sadie asked. Caz looked at her without answering, her eyes slowly travelling over Sadie as though weighing her up. "And you are?" she asked, although her tone was more curious than hostile.

“Special Agent Price, Anchorage FBI,” Sadie said, her new location sounding strange in her mouth. She had been here less than six hours and her day was starting to feel surreal.

Caz raised her eyebrows, which were dyed a shade of red as vibrant as her hair.

“You’ve got the Feds in already?” she said, addressing her question to Cooper rather than to her.

Sheriff Cooper – Sadie couldn’t bring herself to think of him as ‘Logan’ – shrugged. “It wasn’t by request,” he said shortly. Sadie bit her lip to stop herself from retorting, telling herself that this wasn’t the time. She was itching to know what Caz had been sent that had caused Cooper to pull her off from questioning Matthew so quickly. They would have plenty of time to discuss his resentment later.

Caz lifted the wooden hatch that led behind the bar, motioning for them to follow, but as she did so the man that Sadie had recognized decided to speak up.

“Sadie Price? Kyle Price’s daughter? Well, well, well. Does your old man know that you’re a cop now? Can’t see him being too happy with that – you might arrest him for being drunk and disorderly.”

Sadie felt her whole body heat up with shame as his two companions guffawed loudly.

The guy that Sadie remembered from school – Tim, or Tom? Something like that – looked at her and raised his glass in greeting. He looked bloated and red-faced, and Sadie guessed that noontimes in the saloon were a regular occurrence for him.

“You look good Sadie. Even better in cop uniform than you did in your school one. Still got them curves, I see.”

“That’s enough,” Cooper snapped, surprising her. “Watch your manners, the pair of you.”

The older guy rolled his eyes as he placed his glass down on the counter. “Sticking up for the lady, what a hero,” he remarked to no one in particular. Tim or Tom guffawed loudly.

“Are you a lady now, Sadie? Lady Sadie,” he laughed, slurring his words. Drunk before dinnertime. Sadie shook her head in disgust. She was already looking forward to the day when she could once again get the hell out of Alaska.

But she had a few loose ends to tie up first. Not the least finding out the truth about her sister’s death.

“Come on now guys,” Caz said loudly. “The Sherriff and Agent Price here are my guests. How about I pour you another round of drinks on the house and then you clear off? Don't you both have wives to get back to?"

Sadie immediately felt sorry for whichever poor women were at home waiting for such a pair of deadbeats.

Tim – no, Ted, she remembered finally – looked happy as Caz started pouring their drinks. Sadie shared an impatient look with Cooper, who now looked even more pissed off than ever, as though she was personally responsible for the hold up. In his eyes, she supposed she was.

Ted sidled over to her, his breath heavy with whisky. "You investigating the girl found in the lakes then?" he asked. Sadie ignored him, but felt her heart beat faster in her chest as she guessed where this topic was going to lead.

Sure enough, Ted leaned into her, giving her the full force of his breath. "I bet it reminds you of your sister, don't it?" His eyes glinted, as though he was enjoying the effect that he knew his words were likely to have.

"Shut up, Ted," Sadie said through gritted teeth. "You're drunk."

"I'm always drunk," Ted said with a shrug. "Nothing to go home to, see? My wife's as frigid as those lakes. Bet you're not though, ay, Lady Sadie?" He leered at her, his eyes fixed on her breasts, even though her shape was hidden beneath her heavy ski jacket.

The whole bar seemed to be holding its breath. Caz stopped midway through pouring Ted's drink and looked over as Cooper took a step towards Ted. The customers all watched silently, waiting for Sadie's reaction.

"Go away, Ted," Sadie said, sounding bored. She made to turn away from him, dismissing him as though he were no more than a minor annoyance, when to her horror Ted reached for the front of her jacket as though he intended to grab her breasts. From the corner of her eye Sadie saw Cooper reach for his holster.

She was quicker than either of them. Quantico had trained her well, and as a female agent and a petite one at that, Sadie had taken her hand-to-hand combat training seriously. She grabbed Ted's groping fingers with one hand, bending them painfully back, while her other fist made swift contact with the bridge of his nose. There was a satisfying crunch, and Ted screamed as blood ran down his chin.

"She assaulted me!" he yelled, clutching his face. "You all saw it." He motioned around the saloon, but all of the customers seemed to be very interested in their drinks all of a sudden, looking anywhere but in the direction of Ted and Sadie.

"Aren't you going to arrest her?" he yelled at Cooper, who shook his head.

"That looked like a clear-cut case of self-defense to me there, bud," he said evenly. Ted turned appealing eyes to Caz.

"I think it's probably time for you to leave now Ted," the bartender said. "I'll remember your drink for tomorrow."

Ted gave up. Still clutching his nose, he hurried from the saloon, not bothering to look back to his two friends who had moved down to the other side of the bar. The man who knew her father now had his back to her. Sadie took a deep breath and looked at Caz.

"Let's not waste any more time, shall we? Where's this message?"

Looking impressed and more than a little amused, Caz lifted the hatch again and let them through, leading the way to the outhouse behind the bar. Sadie followed, carefully avoiding Cooper's eyes.

It was freezing in the outhouse and Sadie clapped her gloved hands together to warm them. She could see her breath, a tiny curl of smoke in the frigid air.

On a wooden table in the middle of the room sat a block of ice that had been chipped away at on one side. There was something red in the middle of it, sticking out oddly, but at the angle she was looking from Sadie couldn't make out what it was.

"The block was part of a batch order," Caz told them. "We use a local company, so most of the ice is within a fifty-mile radius or so. We order in blocks rather than bags of cubes; it's much cheaper and I can break them up myself, no problem."

Sadie eyed Caz's muscular forearms and didn't doubt the bartender's words.

"Then I saw the flash of red," Caz went on. "As soon as I got the chance this morning I took the pickaxe to it, kept coming in here in between pulling pints to have another go." She looked embarrassed for a moment. "At first, I thought it might even be something valuable. People lose all sorts up here, especially the tourists, you know? But then I realized what it was and, in light of what happened to poor Verity – well, I called it in. It looks like something she might have worn, see?"

"You did the right thing," Cooper said, leaning down and staring at the object embedded in the ice. "We need to get this to the station and find out who it belongs to."

Sadie fought the urge to barge him out of the way so that she could see exactly what they were looking at.

"What is it?"

Cooper stepped out of the way. "I suppose something like this is right up your street," he said grudgingly. "Psychoanalysis and all that. I mean, what if this wasn't an accident?"

"I'm not a therapist," Sadie grumbled as Caz looked at her curiously. It always annoyed her when small town cops confused the realities of her job with what they saw on the CBS channel.

Behavioral analysis consisted of a lot more than profiling potential killers. In the decade since she had become a fully-fledged BAU agent she had been called onto cases across the country to provide investigative support and case management, advise on interrogation and interview techniques, and give expert testimony, as well as the crime and offender analysis usually associated with her role in the popular imagination.

As well as the infamous Boston serial with the penchant for power tools, she had worked on child trafficking rings – always the worst - school shootings and gang crime.

If Cooper thought that she was going to be some kind of pushover, he could think again. Tiredness, hunger, and the idiots in the bar had made Sadie grumpy and impatient to get a lead on this case so she could report back to Golightly and, finally, get some sleep.

She looked at the scarlet object encased in the block and repressed a shudder, thinking of blood on snow. Of other bodies in the ice, back when Sadie had known nothing of killings or any crime worse than a spot of underage drinking.

Her sister's murder had shattered her innocence forever.

Focusing on the object at hand, Sadie raised an eyebrow as she looked at Cooper and then back at the ice block. She understood now why it was being assumed this had something to do with Verity's death.

The object in the ice was a shoe. A woman's shoe, red and pointed, with a killer heel. Half of it was still encased firmly in the ice, as though the block was reluctant to give up its secrets.

"I'll give the ME a call," Cooper said. "He'll need to see this, and to analyze the shoe."

"Is it Verity's?" Caz asked the obvious question that hung in the air. Cooper gave her a sharp look. "How well did you know her, Caz? Was she a regular?"

Caz shrugged. "Some. She didn't talk to me all that much, but I saw her in here most weekends. More since she moved in with Matty. They come in when they are coming down, sit there tweaking in the corner mostly."

"Do you know much about their relationship?" Sadie asked, deliberately keeping her voice casual even though her heart was beating a tattoo in her chest. Matthew had something to do with this, she felt sure of it. Even if he wasn't the killer, he knew a lot more than he was letting on.

"I dunno if you would call it a relationship," Caz was saying, running a plump hand through her short hair. "Rumor was he was pimping her out. That he stole her from Peter Montgomery. You know him?"

"Yes. Was Matthew – Matty – ever violent to Verity, that you know of?"

"Not that I've heard. But the meth heads, they don't come in the saloon at night so much, and nighttime is when it tends to get rowdy. Drinkers and meth heads, they're a different breed. I only tend to see them when their supply has run out or they need to come down a bit. Although with meth, it's easy enough for them to cook up their own, I guess."

"Does Peter do the cooking round here?" Cooper asked, narrowing his eyes. Sadie could tell from their earlier visit that the Sherriff would love to bring Montgomery in, and she couldn't say that she blamed him. Even without the pimping and the drug dealing, Peter was a nasty piece of work.

"Maybe. He certainly sells to most folks as far as I know, and I hear a lot," Caz said, almost proudly.

"But Matthew and Verity had to be getting their meth from elsewhere," Cooper pointed out, lifting up the block as though it barely weighed a gram. "I didn't get the impression they were Peter's friends."

"I don't know," Caz said, and Sadie wanted to believe her. For all of the woman's rough edges, she instinctively liked the bartender. Even so, Sadie wasn't naïve. People rarely told the cops everything, even when they didn't have much of anything to hide.

"Well, if you think of anything else, please let us know. Anything at all. Sometimes the smallest details can turn out to be important," Sadie pressed.

"I will," Caz promised, showing them back out.

As they drove towards the station, Sadie waited for Cooper to lay into her about her failure to disclose the nature of her high school relationship with Matthew. Instead, he surprised her by saying, "You did good in there. It will be a while before any of the locals bother you like that again. Word travels fast round here."

"I can look after myself," Sadie admitted.

"So I see. Right, I'll drop you back to your vehicle, and I'll let you know what happens with the shoe. There are no more real leads right now, so I guess we can split up and do our own research."

Oh no you don't, Sadie thought. As much as she might resent being partnered up with Cooper, she wasn't about to let him push her off the case either, just as Golightly had warned her that he would. She shook her head fiercely. "I'm coming with you," she insisted. "If the shoe turns out to be a calling card, you're going to need me on this."

"I've worked murders before, believe it or not," Cooper said, and she could see the pulse working in his jaw. Clearly the flattery was over, and they were back to the morning's hostilities. Sadie wondered if her show of strength had threatened Cooper as much as it had impressed him. He struck her as a typical local cop, someone who fancied himself as a bit of a hero. She suspected he wasn't used to women rescuing themselves – although on the other hand, his sister could probably break a few balls too.

"Ones where red stilettoes turn up in blocks of ice?" she enquired sweetly.

Cooper grimaced. "Fine," he said, revving the engine.

They drove to the station in silence, but Sadie was past caring what Cooper thought of her. As far as she was concerned, the hunt for the killer was on, and that block of ice held their biggest clue yet.

CHAPTER SEVEN

Sadie was itching to find out what, if anything, the shoe could tell them. Waiting in the main office at the small local station, she was bouncing on the balls of her feet with impatience.

"Do you want a sandwich?" Cooper asked her. She looked at him in surprise. The stubborn part of her wanted to insist that she was fine, thank you, but she felt her stomach grumble again at the mere mention of food.

"Yes, please," she said instead, accepting his offer gratefully.

Sadie looked around as Cooper disappeared into a small kitchen that adjoined the main office. If the Anchorage FBI office had seemed smaller and less grand than she was used to, then this was positively rustic, no more than a few rooms in a large cabin. The single computer on the main desk looked like a relic from the nineties. No wonder Cooper resented her appearance, flashing her shiny Federal badge around when his own division was clearly lacking in funding.

He reappeared and set a steaming mug of coffee and a doorstop of a cheese sandwich in front of her. She tore into it, acutely aware of how empty her stomach was now that she had the opportunity to fill it. As she chased the bread and cheese down with a strong coffee Cooper sat opposite her and she braced herself. She was expecting him to question her about Matthew or, worse, her sister, and so was relieved when he spoke about the shoe instead.

"The ME is on his way. That snow seems to be staying pretty steady at the moment, so it shouldn't take him too long. I hope this is relevant and not some kind of red herring."

Sadie nodded, as she had been thinking the same thing herself. "Although, it would be one hell of a coincidence for a woman's shoe to turn up lodged in recently cut ice right after a woman's body turns up in the lakes. Caz said it looked like something Verity would have worn. I'm guessing it came off with the currents."

"You don't think the killer took it as some form of trophy?" Cooper asked, looking disappointed. "I suppose all that is just a myth; something you only see on TV?"

Sadie took another swig of her drink before answering. "Sadly, it can actually be quite common," she said. "And the taking of trophies denote a certain type of murder. The type of killer who keeps a trophy is killing for kicks. Keeping a trophy is like a souvenir of the event; a reminder of what for the killer may have been a euphoric, even intimate act. So no, it's highly unlikely the killer would have taken a trophy and then deliberately wanted it to be found. Killers who take trophies keep them around; even take them out from time to time and admire them."

Cooper pulled a face as though he was about to be sick. "Like serial killers, you mean. You've dealt with them before?"

"A few," Sadie said, thinking back to the Boston case that Golightly had complimented her on. That particular killer had a penchant for taking snippets of his victim's pubic hair. She decided Cooper was happier not knowing that piece of information. "It's worth pointing out that plenty of serials don't take trophies."

"You're not saying that is what we could have on our hands here?" Cooper asked, looking startled.

"We've got one body," Sadie reminded him. "Like you told me earlier, let's not get ahead of ourselves. However, it would be a good idea to scan the database for similar murders in Alaska, just in case."

She looked away as she voiced the last sentence, not wanting Cooper to see her flinch at the memory of the one case that she knew would certainly show up in the database. A case that was, as yet, unofficially unsolved.

The thought that had been flickering around her mind all day started to catch fire. Her sister's death had been years ago, and although it had been ruled as suspicious, no culprit had ever been found and most people had eventually come to view it as a tragic accident. Only Sadie had insisted, based on a knowing that originated deep in her gut, that her sister had been murdered. But she had been a teenager then, and no-one had listened to her the way they would now. Was it too far out to entertain the possibility that the cases could be linked?

Sadie pressed a hand to her forehead, willing her thoughts to stop. People, unfortunately, did drown up in the lakes every now and then, she reminded herself. They fell in, or thought the ice was thicker than it was, or succumbed to hypothermia. The similarities stopped there. Her sister had been nothing like Verity, in either appearance or lifestyle. Sadie still believed the finger of suspicion pointed squarely at Matthew.

Matthew, who had been so kind to her after Jessica's death.

The women around him had a nasty habit of ending up getting drowned, it seemed.

"Are you all right?" Cooper asked gruffly. "You look as though you've seen a ghost."

"Something like that," Sadie muttered.

Thankfully, the ME arrived then, right before the Sheriff could ask her any more questions.

"Right, where's this block?" he asked, clearly as eager to get down to work as they were.

"I've put it in the small interview room," Cooper told him, and led them both through. The ME got to work with a small drill, the sound of metal against ice loud in the small room

"The body of our victim has been transferred to the morgue in Anchorage," he told them. "The water in her lungs was the same water from the lake," he told them, "So she was drowned in the lakes, although we can't be certain where she was dumped due to movement of the waters. We can't be a hundred percent on time of death, but I would suspect it was within the last few days."

"So, it may not have been premeditated," Cooper said, glancing at Sadie. In spite of his obvious fascination with serial killers, he looked relieved. A straightforward murder was much more within his jurisdiction and would certainly be easier to contemplate than a deranged lunatic who could strike again. If he hadn't already.

The ME shrugged. "That part of it is down to you guys to figure out. I can only report what I find. This is a lucky find though, isn't it, this shoe?"

Cooper nodded. "The odds of it turning up in the saloon ice have to be astronomical."

"Or not," the ME cut in, carefully lifting the shoe from the ice in gloved hands. They both turned to look at him, momentarily puzzled. "It's not Verity's," he explained. "She was a size six. This is a three. No way she would have squeezed herself into it, it would have been agony."

"Okay, back to square one," Cooper said simply, looking frustrated. "It was a red herring after all. It could have been under the lakes for years." He looked annoyed with himself.

Sadie shook her head. "We can't just ignore this," she said. "We need to know whose it is and where it came from. We can't rule out the possibility of it being connected."

"Connected how? You were the one who was so sure that this was accidental."

Sadie looked him straight in the eyes. "There could be another body," she said, and watched him blanch, his olive skin fading momentarily to gray. As much as she didn't want to make herself look a fool in front of the Cooper siblings by leading them off on a wild goose chase, it was a possibility that had to be investigated, and immediately. Better to be wrong than to be right and have acted too late. And besides, it was more likely than Cooper's idea that the shoe had been sent deliberately.

Thankfully Cooper agreed with her, or at least offered no argument. If he wasn't exactly being friendly now, he at least seemed to be treating her with more respect and less suspicion.

She wondered how long that would last.

"We can find out where the ice came from," Cooper said. "That should give us a starting point at least. I'll radio through to the Deputy and get her to double check there have been no young women in the area reported missing in the last few weeks. It's possible that we've missed something. We also need to know what she has managed to find out about Verity. The girl must have had family somewhere."

He started to bag up the shoe for the ME, who would take it back to Anchorage for testing. Sadie knew that, up here, it could take at least a few days for any results.

There was always the possibility that the owner of the shoe was still alive…but far from safe. Held captive, in fact. Sadie had dealt with too many criminal minds over the years to not automatically run through all possible scenarios, with the worst usually being, in her experience, the most likely to be the case.

She couldn't ignore the gnawing feeling in her stomach that this was going to be bad.

That Verity was just the first.

"There's an old ice harvester up at the gorge, just north of the lakes," Cooper said. Sadie nodded, vaguely remembering the shop from childhood. Her father had visited there occasionally, when he had been sober enough to take notice of anything but the booze. "Mostly retired now, especially after the big companies moved in. But he should be able to tell us where the ice came from. We can send it for analyzing, but that could take weeks at this time of year."

Sadie was heading towards the door before Cooper had even finished his sentence.

"We need to go and talk to him then," she said, her focus now solely on the owner of the shoe and the thought of a young woman in danger. Perhaps this one she could save from an icy death.

"Now," she added.

CHAPTER EIGHT

As they drove past the lakes, Sadie was glad that the still falling snow was thick enough to obscure her view. She was trying not to visualize a second body.

Or to think about Jessica again.

They passed her snowmobile, now thoroughly hemmed in on either side by snowbanks, and Sadie decided it would be a good time to call Golightly.

She gave him very brief details and apologized for the snowmobile. "I'll have to dig it out later. Hopefully the snow will ease up."

"Not much chance of that," her new boss replied gruffly. "I reckon they will be issuing a blizzard warning soon enough. You want to watch that you don't get stuck up there. Especially with the holidays coming up."

"I'll be fine," Sadie assured him, hoping that was true. It wasn't as though she had any plans for Christmas dinner. "I'm sure there are other motels around if I can't get back into Anchorage."

"Okay Price, keep me updated," Golightly told her before ringing off abruptly. Sadie cut the call and saw Cooper looking at her curiously.

"Are you not staying with family or friends?" Cooper asked as she replaced her phone into her pocket.

"No," she said shortly. While he might have had a justifiable reason to be angry at her lack of disclosure before, the Sheriff wasn't entitled to her family background. Sadie hoped he would take her reticence as answer enough and drop that particular line of questioning.

He didn't.

"Is there anything else I need to know about you?" he asked bluntly. Sadie felt her defenses go up even further. "Such as?"

He shrugged without taking his eyes off the road. "I don't know, but I don't want to question any other potential suspects and find out that you have some kind of attachment to them. What did Ted mean about your sister?"

"My sister died when she was a teenager," Sadie said, feeling her mouth go dry. "So no, there is no relevance to this case."

"Fair enough," Cooper said. His voice was softer, expressing sympathy, but Sadie didn't want pity. She just wanted him to stop prying.

Even if he was right, she probably should disclose the circumstances of Jessica's death. If he checked the database far enough back, then it would come up anyway. But there was no realistic way that they could be connected.

Was there?

What if Jessica's killer – assuming there was one – had simply been biding his time? It happened; plenty of serial killers had gaps between their early victims, sometimes because they were inside for other crimes. It had been Sadie who had located the Boston killer's first victim, seven years before the case that had made the headlines and triggered off a spate of killings over a two-year period. This could be the same.

Or even worse, she thought, the killer could have been active for years but stayed under the radar. People like Verity went missing all the time, and often their absence was neither missed nor reported. And these lakes could hide bodies for years…

An icy hand gripped her gut at the thought, and she felt her heart fluttering rapidly in her chest even as her inner, rational voice urged her to calm down. There was no evidence of a serial killer yet. No matter how eerie the sending of the shoe was. Even two bodies, if that was what they found, did not make a serial. The likelihood was these were drug deaths or were related to Verity's prostitution. And there had never been any conclusive evidence for Jessica having been murdered.

Even if Sadie had always been certain of it, with a bone deep instinct that had never left her. It was the same instinct that had made her such a good cop.

The instinct that right now, was telling her that the owner of the shoe was already dead. That no matter how valiantly Cooper wrestled his jeep through the ever-thickening snow, it was going to be too late.

"Is that why you moved away?" Cooper asked, cutting through her thoughts. He sounded genuinely interested and his earlier hostility had softened. The shoe had shaken him.

"Among other reasons," Sadie said evasively. She had no desire to discuss her past with Sherriff Logan Cooper or anyone else, but neither did she want to seem rude just as the atmosphere between them was beginning to thaw. To distract him, she turned the questions on him.

"How about you? Have you always lived and worked in Alaska?"

"Pretty much," he said. "We're from Juneau originally; my dad was a State Trooper there; he retired just last year. I started off there and was moved up here a few years ago. I recruited my sister Jane five years ago after she dropped out of medical school. I can't say that I ever expected her to make Deputy, but she turned out to be a natural. Needless to say, our father is ecstatic that we both ended up following in his footsteps. It worries the hell out of my mom though."

Sadie couldn't help a twinge of jealousy at the family picture he painted. She could imagine the Cooper family sitting around the table at Thanksgiving, taking turns to carve the turkey.

Sadie had worked every Thanksgiving for the last ten years, out of choice. Better that than sitting in by herself with a microwave meal and a bottle of Bud. There had been boyfriends, but no one that she had ever wanted to share Thanksgiving dinner with.

"You sister certainly seems keen," Sadie said, wincing as her words came out sounding more acerbic than she had meant them to.

"I reckon she's got her eyes on my job," Cooper said with a grin. "Sibling rivalry, and all that." It was his turn to wince as he realized what he had said. "I'm sorry…about your sister."

"It's okay," Sadie said quickly. She changed the subject before he could start asking questions again. "This ice harvester, do you know him? I didn't recognize the name."

"We've met a few times," Cooper nodded. "He had a stolen vehicle a few years back. He has a good snowplow too, which has come in useful from time to time. Seems a solid sort of guy, knows his stuff. Which means he will hopefully be able to help us."

"Let's hope so."

Sadie stared out of the window as they turned onto a small track that led up to the ice harvester's shop. Cooper's jeep groaned as it battled against the deepening snow, which was still falling steadily. It wasn't a blizzard yet, but if it continued and the wind picked up, it wouldn't be far from it. Sadie hoped she wasn't about to get stranded out here on her first day on the job. She was desperate for a warm bed and a decent night's sleep.

Once they had found out who the owner of this shoe was.

The ice harvester's place had its blinds firmly down even though the sign on the door said 'Open,' as though the owner was only begrudgingly inviting customers. Cooper unstrapped the block of ice from the top of the snowcat and carried it to the shop, with Sadie close behind.

As they stepped inside, Sadie blinked against the shadows; there was a very little light and the small space was crowded with equipment and dusty shelves of even dustier books.

There was no one behind the small desk, and Cooper rang the bell that sat in the middle of the wooden counter loudly.

A wiry, middle-aged man came out of a door at the back of the shop, peering at them through the dingy light. His slightly sharp features brightened as he saw Cooper.

"Sheriff, nice to see you. This is unusual, I must say." He looked at the half-broken block of ice that Cooper now set on the counter in front of him and his eyes shone with interest. "What do we have here?"

"We need to know where this came from, Mac. Can you help?"

Mac bent down and studied the ice block carefully. Sadie wondered what it was he could see that the average person wouldn't. As far as she was concerned, ice was ice.

Ice harvesting, or cutting as it was usually known, was rare these days, a niche skill in the days of mechanical refrigeration and air conditioning. In parts of Alaska however it was seen as something of a local skill, and there were still a few traditionalists and hobbyists who practiced the art of collecting surface ice from the lakes and gorges in the winter to be used for storage and cooling in the – somewhat – warmer summer months. Clearly Mac was something of an expert.

"I hope so," he said. "Any ideas at all where it came from?"

"Only that we are pretty sure its local," Sadie said. Mac nodded without looking at her, engrossed in studying patterns only he could see.

"Can I cut a strip off?" the ice harvester asked Cooper. "I've got some in the icehouse out back I would like to compare it to."

"Whatever you need," Cooper shrugged.

The harvester got to work with a small saw specifically designed for the task, before going back out of the door. Sadie rubbed her hands together and stamped her feet, as much with impatience as with cold. She was glad when Mac reappeared only a few minutes later, nodding his head wisely.

"It's from the freshwater lakes up at the gorge," he told them. "The water inlets up there are the freshest in the valley; that's how we can identify it. You're in luck."

Sadie and Cooper exchanged a glance. The gorge was a few miles north, further into the wilderness than the fishing lakes where they had found Verity. It was also going into Inuit territory.

"It's fairly deserted round those parts," Cooper said.

"There's an Inuit guy who lives up at the gorge," Mac said. "A trapper and furrier. Does a pretty good trade. Whatever you're looking for up there, he might be able to help."

Cooper looked at Sadie.

"I guess that's our next stop then," he said.

"I'd be careful up there, though," Mac went on. "He's not always the friendliest of guys to outsiders, or so I've heard. And it's a treacherous kind of place. A lot of people have gone missing up in the gorge over the years."

Sadie felt a shiver go through her that had nothing to do with the temperature, as she wondered just how much the trapper knew.

*

As they drove, Sadie thought back to what she knew about the Inuit people of Alaska. The Inuit were an indigenous people who had inhabited not just the frozen wilds of Alaska but had also migrated across to Canada, Siberia, and Greenland, living in those territories undisturbed for millennia before the arrival of Europeans. Once known as 'Eskimos,' the term was now considered inappropriate, a relic of colonialist stereotypes, although some Inuit peoples had reclaimed the word for themselves.

The Inuit of Alaska had, in many areas, tried their best to hold on to their Native traditions, often in the face of persecution from settlers and successive US and Canadian policies. Like Native Americans across the continent, they still suffered from racism and inequality.

Sadie remembered the few Inuit kids who had been in her classes at primary school, who had mostly kept themselves to themselves. They had been easy targets for bullies like Peter Montgomery, who had particularly harassed the Inuit girls.

The community north of Anchorage, like many First Nations peoples, were tight knit and didn't tend to mix with local non-Natives or the towns folk of Anchorage. In recent years there had been a push towards reviving Native languages and customs, and even teaching about them in mainstream schools. Sadie doubted that the occasional nod towards multiculturalism and RE lesson about festivals was going to do much to make up for centuries of persecution, but she supposed it was a start.

"You know this guy?" she asked Cooper. She shook his head.

"No. Honestly, I don't know anyone in the Inuit community here as well as I should, but then making connections hasn't been easy. They have a settled land claim and a self-governing agreement, so they tend to police themselves, and are distrustful of local non-Native law enforcement. I suppose we can't blame them, so I haven't tried to muscle my way in. There has never been any need; they don't tend to be the guys causing any of the trouble."

"So, if this trapper has heard or seen anything, he's unlikely to tell us," Sadie said with a sigh. Mac being able to give them a location for the ice block so quickly had been a boost, but now she wondered if they were about to hit a dead end.

"Let's wait and see. I mean, we can't rule him out as a suspect yet, not until we've spoken to him," Cooper said.

Sadie saw what must be the trapper's lodge emerge out of the blanket whiteness in front of them, to the left of the frozen gorge. It was a small, triangle shaped building on stilts, the roof jutting out over the front of the cabin, loaded with snow. It looked as though it had seen better days and could potentially collapse any moment, its fragility in stark contrast to the mountains that reared up behind, majestic in their strength.

As a kid, she had often thought that living in the wilds of Alaska must seem like living in Narnia to those who lived in sunnier climates, but of course it hadn't been a fairytale at all. No Aslan had come along to save Jessica or Verity, or the mysterious owner of the red shoe.

There was no-one around and no sign of a dog sled as they got out of the jeep a few hundred yards away and trekked up towards the lodge. There was a bitter breeze coming down from the mountains. Sadie remembered Golightly's warnings about an impending blizzard and felt herself shudder at the thought of being trapped all the way up here.

At least she wasn't alone. She glanced over at Cooper, wondering how long they could be stranded together for before they drove each other mad.

He knocked on the door of the lodge and they waited for a good few minutes before he knocked again, louder this time, but there was still nothing. Sadie leaned towards the thick wooden door, listening for any signs of life.

"No one home," Cooper said with an impatient sigh. "Now what?"

“Let’s have a look around,” she said, not wanting to give up.

Sadie started to walk around the lodge, calling to Cooper when she saw a small outhouse with the door slightly ajar. “Over here,” she yelled. Cooper followed her and Sadie rapped on the open door and then, when there was no answer, she pushed it fully open and stepped inside.

The strong, musty scent of fur and long dead carcasses hit her, and she heaved, then quickly stifled the sound as Cooper came in behind her. As they looked around, she realized that the place looked deserted, as though nothing had been touched for some time. The pelts that hung from the ceiling, nearest to the door, had a thin layer of frost over them.

“Ooof, it smells a bit in here,” Cooper complained as he started to walk around the outhouse. “These pelts look fairly old, too.”

“I didn’t see any sled tracks around,” Sadie said, “although the snow today could have covered a lot.”

Cooper stood still, scanning the shed. “To be honest, I’m thinking our guy cleared off some time ago,” he said, the disappointment obvious in his voice. “Most of these hooks are empty; he’s probably taken the best pelts with him.”

“We don’t know that. I’ll go and knock at the cabin again.”

Sadie trudged through the snow back around to the front of the cabin and knocked the door loudly. Again, there was no answer. She looked away over the small lake. A shadow on the surface caught her eye and she felt the icy hand twisting her gut again as she made out its shape and size. She left the cabin and walked towards the lake, half willing herself to be wrong.

But there, on the surface near the edge was a perfectly cut square that looked to be the exact same size as the block when they had first seen it at the saloon. There were no other areas where ice had been harvested, just that one missing piece.

“Cooper!” Sadie yelled, her voice echoing out over the silent gorge. “We might have found where the shoe came from.”

She didn’t voice the rest of that thought, but it raced around in her mind as she continued to stare at the broken surface.

If they had found the original location of the shoe, then they might also have found the foot that fitted it. Sadie inched herself out onto the ice, ignoring Cooper’s shout of warning behind her, and peered into the gap.

The snow and the depth of the water beneath her made it hard to be certain, but as Sadie stared into the lake, she was sure that she caught a flash of something. She leaned forward.

"Agent Price!" Cooper yelled behind her. "Be careful!"

Sadie sucked in her breath. There was no mistaking it something floated in the depths below her.

It was red.

She made her way back to the side of the lake. Cooper took one look at her face and wasted no time in reaching for his radio.

"Deputy," he barked into the microphone. "We need a dive and search team." He paused to listen to the response and then said in a flat voice, "Immediately. We might have found another body."

CHAPTER NINE

Sadie stamped her feet impatiently as she scanned the sky overhead for any sign of the chopper.

"Are you okay?" Cooper asked, dragging his gaze away from the cut-out in the lake. Sadie could imagine how dark his thoughts were.

She shared them.

"Yes, just cold and impatient," she said. Cooper nodded.

"You and me both. Jane just texted; they're close. Luckily the lake isn't one of the bigger ones. If there's anything - anyone – there, it won't take them long to find."

"This is the part I hate," Sadie said, almost talking to herself. "The searching. Is there a body or isn't there? Is it related or not? Wanting to find something so that you know what you're dealing with and are hopefully closer to catching the perp, but knowing that if you do, it means another person dead."

"You must have worked a lot of cases like this. It's tough. Any senseless loss of life, it wears me down," Cooper confided. For a moment any animosity between them had subsided as they sat waiting to find out what may lie underneath the ice.

It wasn't like Sadie to be so morbid on a case; she prided herself on being pragmatic. On getting the job done. But this wasn't just any case. She had known that returning would bring the memories of Jessica flooding back…but not like this. There was no way that she could have anticipated this.

The sound of a helicopter came from overhead, interrupting her chain of thought, and they both got to their feet as they waited for the dive team to land near the lake.

Deputy Cooper emerged from the chopper first and made her way over to them, shooting Sadie a dirty look as she did so. Sadie kept her face deliberately neutral, but inside she felt herself bristle with annoyance. She had more than proved her worth today. They needed her on this. Clearly the Deputy resented that fact.

"How likely is it that there's even a body here?" she asked, and although her eyes were on her brother, judging by her snarky tone Sadie knew that the question was aimed at her.

"Given that the mysterious block of ice came from here, and it contained a woman's shoe, just after we've discovered a body in a similar lake? I think we all know the answer to that," Sadie said calmly. The Deputy didn't answer, preferring to act as though she hadn't heard her. If she wanted to ignore her, she could live with that, Sadie thought. She was rapidly running out of patience with the other woman's undisguised hostility.

"Unless the killer – assuming that's who it is – is sending us on a wild goose chase," Cooper said. Sadie grimaced.

"It happens. What still bothers me about all this though, is why send the block to the saloon, why not to the station? If it's the attention of the people trying to catch him that he wants, then it makes no sense – not yet, anyway." A second body would possibly reveal more.

Sadie walked away from the Coopers, around the edge of the lake, to get a closer look at the dive and search team as they began their operation. She hoped they had brought a body bag.

She stood there for a while, arms folded against the cold, poised for a signal that something had been found, while Sheriff Cooper and his sister chatted away in low voices behind her. At some point the afternoon had turned into evening and she was beyond tired now, instead her whole body was thrumming with an unpleasant wired feeling.

A sense of foreboding hung over the lake, mirrored by the gathering, darkening clouds, heavy with snow. They rolled in across the mountains, bringing the threat of more extreme weather with them, and Sadie couldn't help but shudder, reading them as an omen of more than simply snow.

What else was coming?

The light, gloomy to start with, was fading rapidly and inky shadows were making their way across the surface of the lake. Daylight didn't last long here, especially in the winter months. Some parts of the North had no light at all this time of year but lived in a perpetual darkness. Sadie pulled her ski jacket more tightly around herself, willing the search team to work faster. She couldn't go another night without a decent sleep, but she also knew that she was going nowhere until the lake had been fully dragged. If she had to stand here all night, blizzard or no blizzard, she would do it.

Then Cooper called to her.

"Do you want a coffee, Price? Deputy Cooper brought a flask."

Sadie walked gratefully over to them. "A stiff whiskey would be more in order, but coffee will do," she quipped. Cooper smiled, acknowledging the joke, but the Deputy raised a sardonic eyebrow.

"That's more your father's bag, isn't it?" she said, smirking. "Drinking, I mean. I heard he used to be a regular at some of the saloons himself."

"Heard that where?" Sadie snapped. The Deputy shrugged, a deliberately casual movement that infuriated Sadie. She was in no mood for this.

"Word gets around fast, especially around these parts. But there's plenty of old alcoholics around here. What I did find interesting, Agent Price, is your potential conflict of interest in this case."

Sadie looked at Cooper, guessing he had filled his sister in on her past relationship with their prime suspect. Even though Cooper owed her no loyalty, she still felt stung.

"If you're talking about Matthew…" she began, then stopped as she saw the look of confusion on the Deputy's face.

"Who? No, Price, I'm talking about your sister."

Sadie felt herself freeze at the mention of Jessica. She didn't want to talk about her sister to the Deputy, and especially not here and now, with another body potentially about to be dragged out of the lakes.

"Jane," Cooper said, his voice a quiet warning to back off. His sister ignored him; her eyes were boring into Sadie's.

"It seems odd, doesn't it?" the Deputy said. "Your sister drowns in a frozen lake in suspicious circumstances, and you take off just as soon as you're grown. Then you arrive back here just as bodies start turning up in lakes again."

Sadie felt her blood begin to boil. "Just exactly what the fuck," she said through gritted teeth, stepping towards the other woman, "are you trying to say?"

"Whoa," the Sheriff cut in, perhaps fearing for his sister's nose after the incident at the saloon. "Knock it off, the pair of you. This isn't helping anything."

Sadie stepped back, shoving her hands in her pockets. They had balled into fists involuntarily.

"It's a fair comment," the Deputy insisted, clearly not knowing when to shut up. "If this has personal connotations for Agent Price, may even possibly be related for all we know, then her professional judgment could be compromised. We should at least ask for a different agent to be assigned to this case."

Cooper didn't answer and again, Sadie felt stung, knowing that he was possibly thinking along the same lines, and why wouldn't he? She would say the same in their situation; she had reassigned agents before when cases hit too close to home for them to keep a clear mind.

"But that wasn't all you were saying," she snapped instead. "You may as well have outright accused me of having something to do with it."

The Deputy shrugged again, and Sadie clenched her hands so hard she wondered if her nails would draw blood on her palms.

"It's just a mighty coincidence, that's all I'm saying," the woman said. There was a smirk playing on her lips. She knew that she had rattled Sadie, and she was enjoying it. Sadie fought to keep control of her temper.

"Why are you even here?" she challenged. "This is way above your pay grade, which is probably why you're coming out with such inane comments. Don't you have a trespasser to catch or something?"

Deputy Cooper's mouth fell open, enraged, and she was about to retort in return when a shout came over to them from the dive team.

They rushed over to see what was being hauled through the ice, and Sadie's anger faded to nothing, to be replaced by a dawning horror.

The body of a young woman with long, dark hair came to the surface.

She was wearing a red dress.

CHAPTER TEN

Earlier that afternoon, he had driven up a residential street on the outskirts of Anchorage, driving slowly because of the snow, which was ever-present these days.

It was fine by him. He liked the snow. There were less people around, and the world was quieter, and cleaner somehow. He liked that too; there was so much that wasn't clean. Women, especially, hiding their filth under a pretty smile or a pretty dress.

Like the red dress that the whore had worn, an appropriate color for her, of course. Signaling who and what she was like a beacon, designed to entice men in. Fools, all of them.

But he wasn't a fool, and the whore's pretty smile had soon turned into tears as she had begged for her life, pleading with him not to hurt her.

He liked it when they did that. It gave him a sense of power, but something more than that, too. It gave him clarity.

Purpose. He had done a good thing, ridding the world of their filth. Of their seductive charms that enticed and repulsed at the same time, entrapping lesser men and making them no better than slaves.

He was better than that. He was more powerful than that, and by the time he had finished with them, the whores had known that, and the world was free of a little less filth.

A school bus turned the corner in front of him, forcing him to slow down even more. He tutted, drumming his fingers on the wheel with impatience. He cursed as the bus moved in front of him, trapping him behind it as both vehicles crawled up the road.

It was a nice road, tree-lined, with houses on either side. If it wasn't for all the snow, one could be anywhere in Middle America, in a nice suburban neighborhood where men watered the lawn on the weekend while their wives entertained visitors.

It was a world that he had known, once, and then discarded. Stupid people with their stupid, irritating habits and routines, not even an inkling of what it was to truly be free.

The bus pulled over in front of him and he was about to overtake it when a group of girls, identical in their school blazers, caught his attention.

Or rather, one of them did. She had long, dark hair and the kind of features that so enticed him. Like the whores, but she was different.

Younger. Fresher. She looked like a senior, maybe seventeen or eighteen. He wondered if she was still innocent and uncorrupted.

Probably not. Not in this day and age. They were all whores, in the end.

He watched her wave to her friends and walk towards one of the houses, looking down at her phone. That annoyed him. No one was ever present in the moment anymore. Brainwashed, stupid fools.

He should have driven away, but he felt compelled to watch her. Could she be the next one to come to him?

The thought made his heart beat faster in his chest. She was different than the whores, which made her all the more potent as prey. She wouldn't taunt him or try to seduce him. She would appreciate and understand his power.

He could take his time with her. Watch the waters closing over her slowly, and the life draining from her eyes. Unlike the whores, she didn't need cleaning. Instead, he could keep her clean forever.

The thought gave him a rush, one that was more than sexual. He had transcended such things. This was a higher purpose.

A horn sounded behind him, and he realized that he was now blocking the road. He drove on, taking his eyes off the girl just before she disappeared into her house.

He knew where she lived.

It was only a matter of time, and she would be his.

CHAPTER ELEVEN

Sadie tried not to show her emotions as she looked at the girl's dead body on the slab in front of her. The Medical Examiner – who, Sadie had finally learned, was called Pete – pursed his lips as he surveyed it. His gaze seemed almost cold to Sadie, sweeping over the corpse as though it was no more than an object on the slab, which she supposed to him, it was. This was his job.

It was her job, too, and Sadie had seen her fair share of bodies over the years. Mostly, they had stopped bothering her, unless they had been killed in a particularly gruesome way, or it was a child. The minors were always tough, to the point that even if she ever met a man that she felt able to settle down with, Sadie was adamant that she didn't want children. She had seen firsthand just how many horrors the world held, and how it was impossible to keep someone truly and completely safe.

Monsters hid in every corner.

This body bothered her, though. It was her second in one day, and the bloated face, its expression frozen into one of horror, would haunt her dreams that night. It was impossible to look at the girl's face and not see her screaming in terror as the unknown assailant snuffed out her life.

Sadie wondered, not for the first time, if Jessica had screamed. Had known that she was dying. A pain that was old enough to be familiar gnawed at Sadie's guts, asking for acknowledgment. But Sadie would be burned alive before she would show any emotion in front of Deputy Cooper. And so, her face remained as outwardly passive as the examiners.

"Do we know who she is?"

Pete shook his head. "No. I've sent her DNA to the lab and marked it 'Urgent,' but it will be tomorrow before we hear anything, and that's if we're lucky. She may not even show up in the database; Verity didn't."

Someone had to know her, Sadie thought. Someone had to be missing her. Again, she thought of Jessica, and those hours when they had been searching for her, not knowing where she was. When Sadie had been expecting her to turn up safe and sound.

Instead, she had turned up like this. On a slab in the morgue, frozen and bloated.

"As with the first vic," Pete went on, "time of death is going to be next to impossible to determine, thanks to the ice. This killer knows what they are doing in that respect."

"It's definitely murder then," Sadie said, almost to herself. A statement, rather than a question. She had already known, but needed it confirmed. This killer, she swore, she would bring to justice.

"Same MO as before," Pete said. "Those pressure marks on her chest indicate she was held down. She drowned in the lake; the water in her lungs came from there."

"So, he's killing and dumping at the same site," Cooper said.

"Yes, but he could be holding them beforehand. Without any missing reports or times of death, we don't really have any indication of just what is going on here."

The Deputy looked up at Sadie's words. "You're the expert," she said, not even bothering to hide her sneer. "Surely you have some idea?"

Sadie ignored her, not even looking at her or acknowledging her comment. After the Deputy's attempt to bait her about her sister, Sadie had decided the best course of action, if she wasn't going to end up breaking two noses in one day, was just to pretend that the other woman wasn't there. Instead, she turned to Pete.

"The shoe?" she said quietly. She needed to check, even if she instinctively knew the answer.

Almost reverently, Pete picked up the shoe which Cooper had brought back out of Evidence and eased it onto the girl's foot. Its bright hue looked almost mocking against the blue, waxy skin.

"A little tight, but her feet are swollen. I would guess it fit her plenty well enough before."

"It would help if we knew where the other one was," Cooper said. "The dive team carried on after we left, just in case there was anything else. I'll radio through and see if they've found it. Or do you think," he asked Sadie, "that he kept the second one as his trophy?"

"If it isn't in the lake, then I would say it is a possibility."

The Deputy went white as she looked between Sadie and her brother. For once, when she spoke to Sadie, there was no snark or hostility in her voice. Just fear.

"Trophy? Are we talking serial killer here?"

Sadie sighed heavily, rubbing her brow. The tiredness was suddenly threatening to overwhelm her, and her thoughts felt disconnected, scattering around in her mind.

"Technically, more than two bodies are needed for a serial," she said, her voice flat. "And without knowing who our second victim is, we don't know what connects her and Verity. Statistically, this is more likely to be related to drugs and prostitution, given Verity's recent circumstances."

"This one has similar burns on her fingers too," Cooper noted, leaning forward to look. Sadie nodded.

"So, she's another meth user, which likely means that she and Verity knew each other. So, as I said, we are most likely looking at drugs-related killings here. The anomaly, of course, is the method of the killings. If these are just drug deaths, why not just shoot them? And leave the bodies where they would be found as a warning? The way they've been drowned, held down under the ice, there's something almost intimate about that. Something personal. Even if this was over drugs, the killer either knew the girls personally or there is something else about them that got his goat."

"They look alike," Cooper said. Sadie nodded again. There was something about both girls that was bothering her, but she couldn't put her finger on what it was. She was too exhausted, and as she continued it became an effort to put the words together. Her voice sounded monotonous to her, devoid of emotion.

"They do. We need to know who our second vic is. If she is – was – a prostitute like Verity, then that might well be the link. We need to question Peter and Matthew again. Get a list of johns. If we are looking at a serial...well, prostitutes are a common target, especially at first."

Cooper raised an eyebrow. "At first?"

"Yes. It's happened in a few high-profile cases. They are easy to target and often their deaths go unnoticed. What's another missing hooker? That's how society views these girls." A note of compassion slipped into her voice, and she couldn't help but glance at the dead girl's face. A strand of dark hair fell over her forehead and Sadie had the sudden urge to brush it off her face. To tell the girl everything would be okay.

Even though that would be a lie. Nothing was going to be okay for her and Verity ever again, just like it hadn't been for Jessica. Sadie couldn't take that back.

But she could find their killer, and hopefully before he did this to any other poor girl. For all Sadie's cautious words about drug killings to the Coopers, her gut told her otherwise.

Whoever killed these girls hated them and everything that they represented.

"So, often a serial will begin with them and then move on to other demographics," she went on. "What can start off as a hatred towards women seen as dirty, or outcast, often boils down to a hatred of all women. And the rush of getting away with it makes the killer brave. It's like a substance addiction – tolerance for the high of the kill develops. So, they need to take bigger risks, target more visible victims. If this is about what they look like, sooner or later all dark-haired young women could be a target."

Cooper whistled under his breath. "Let's hope we are just dealing with a drug gang incident, then," he said. "We'll question Peter and Matthew again."

"And Caz," Sadie insisted. "If our first victim frequented the saloon, then it has to be a safe bet that our second did, too. It may even be where they met the killer."

"Maybe the saloon was being used as a place to do drug deals?" Deputy Cooper piped up. "And these girls pissed someone off – possibly Peter? I bet he would have counted the saloon as his exclusive turf."

"Again, it's possible. Maybe even the most likely scenario."

"But you don't really think that do you?" Cooper said. His voice was quiet. Sadie met his eyes.

"No," she said. "I don't. But I could be wrong."

"Well, as long as your judgment isn't being clouded by your past," the Deputy sniped. Sadie had wondered how long it would be before the woman started again. She was a liability.

"Either way," Sadie ignored her and addressed Cooper. "We need to speak to Peter."

"And we will," he said. "And Matthew, and Caz. Tomorrow."

Sadie opened her mouth to protest, but Cooper shook his head resolutely.

"There's no more that we can do today, and nothing more that we can do for these girls. It's full dark out, and well below freezing. We're done for today. And even if we weren't - you need to get some sleep."

Sadie wanted to protest that he couldn't tell her what to do, but she knew that he was right. Exhaustion was catching up to her fast and if she really wanted to get justice for these girls then she needed to be awake and on the ball.

"Okay," she said instead, with as much dignity as she could muster.

"I'll help you dig out your snowcat. Get you both back in one piece or your boss Golightly will make my life hell," Cooper grinned. Sadie appreciated his attempt at brevity, was touched by it even, but she barely had the energy to muster a smile. She said goodbye to Pete, nodded curtly at Deputy Cooper, and followed the Sheriff outside.

The sooner she got some sleep, the sooner she could get back on the case.

Something was bothering her about the empty furrier's shack, though. They still needed to speak to him. There was still something niggling at her about the whole case, and she needed to know what it was. For some reason she felt it might be connected to the furrier, although in what way she wasn't sure.

Maybe she could take the long way back, around past the gorge, just in case he had returned.

*

It was so dark outside that the only illumination was her headlights. The snow was still steadily falling, and Sadie knew that she needed to get back to Anchorage and onto better roads before she got stuck.

Or fell asleep at the wheel. Her limbs felt like lead, as though her body had fallen asleep while she was still awake. She dragged herself out of the vehicle and made her way to the furrier's cabin.

But the place was as deserted as it had been earlier, and Sadie got back into the snow plough feeling foolish. She drove back down to the main road when something in the headlights caught her eye. There were tire tracks going up the other side of the gorge, and a path she hadn't noticed before. She hesitated for only a moment before following the tracks.

They led her a short way through the pines to a dead end. A chain-link fence under which the tire tracks continued. A large padlock kept the gates shut. Beyond that she couldn't see.

Sadie turned off her lights and pulled her torch out of her backpack. Bracing herself against the cold, she stepped out of the snow plough and swept her torch across the gates to illuminate what lay behind them. Seeing a building and a car she stepped forward, pushing her face up to the fence.

The path turned into a large driveway in which a long, black SUV was parked. Behind it stood a log manor house, the richest looking building she had seen around the area. It looked new, and she certainly didn't remember it from childhood. Not that she had ever really come up this way.

She shone her torchlight on the SUV, preparing to memorize the number plate.

It wouldn't be difficult. Two words, GODS WORK, shone in the torchlight. Whoever lived in the manor was religious enough to want to very obviously advertise it everywhere they went.

Sadie shivered with more than just cold. It wouldn't be the first time that sex workers had been targeted by those who thought they were a stain on God's creation. Given the proximity of this house to the gorge, she needed to know who lived there.

Back in her vehicle, she radioed Cooper.

"Price." He sounded concerned. "You get back okay?"

"I'm up at the gorge," she said, and quickly continued before he could attempt to chew her out. "There's a large manor house here. Recent tracks leading into it. Black SUV, number plate GODS WORK. You know it?"

There was a pause. "Yes," Cooper said, sounding more than a little annoyed. "It belongs to Elijah Sutcliffe. *Reverend* Elijah Sutcliffe. He's the town preacher up at Anchorage Baptist church."

That made him no less likely to be a suspect in Sadie's eyes. "Is he clean?"

"Yes," Cooper said, sounding exasperated now. "You're suggesting I suspect the *preache*r just because he lives in the vicinity?"

"If you had worked on some of the cases I have, Sheriff, you wouldn't rule out anyone," Sadie said.

"Fine," he said flatly, and Sadie realized that he may have taken her comment as a dig at his expertise. "Now, will you GO AND GET SOME SLEEP."

The radio went silent.

Sadie drove off, squinting at the road ahead. She felt silly, now. Worried that Cooper would see her as overzealous, and that his sister had been right. That Sadie wouldn't be able to work this case effectively, given the circumstances of her sister's death. She had little doubt that Cooper was thinking the same thing even if he hadn't yet said that.

She wondered if Golightly would share their view.

By the time she reached the motel, grateful to be able to drive at something more than a crawl when she reached the gritted main roads of Anchorage, her eyes were barely open.

The motel looked small and unwelcoming, its exterior paint peeling and the 'No Vacancies' sign hanging by a rusty chain. Sadie fumbled under the mat for the key, turned it in the lock and stumbled up the stairs after hanging the key on a hook near the coat rack. The interior was as shabby as outside, with a threadbare carpet and the smell of tobacco smoke, but Sadie was past caring.

She located Room 5, where she had been told she had been put, opened the door and threw her backpack and coat on a chair near the bed. Then she bolted the door, pulled off her clothes and left them in a heap on the floor before climbing into the bed. It creaked beneath her, and she felt the springs digging through the material.

Her eyelids fluttered once and then closed. She drifted off, wondering what fresh horrors tomorrow would bring.

CHAPTER TWELVE

Sadie opened her eyes, instantly awake as she heard footsteps next to her bed.

There was someone in her room. She tried to sit up, to scream, to reach for her gun, but her body was still paralyzed with sleep, and she could neither move nor talk. The footsteps got louder, but then moved away towards the other side of the room.

Somehow, Sadie managed to turn her head to see a shadowy figure bending over her sister's bed, where Jessica lay sleeping soundly. Sadie tried to scream again, to warn her, but once again nothing came out. She had to help Jessica, but she couldn't move.

Jessica woke up and started screaming herself as the figure dragged her from her bed, across the room and out of the door.

"No!" Sadie cried, finally finding her voice. She found her movement too, sitting up and swinging her legs out of the bed. As she looked down at herself, she saw her pink nightshirt and her thin, fifteen-year-old legs. She was a girl again.

And her sister needed her.

She ran, following the figure and Jessica, out of the house and down a snowy hillside. She could see them in the distance, Jessica struggling to no avail and screaming loudly as she desperately attempted to get free of her captor. Sadie ran, but her skinny legs couldn't catch up. She saw something gleaming at the bottom of the hill, moonlight striking its smooth surface.

The lakes. He was taking Jessica to the lakes.

Sadie screamed as loudly as she could, but the sound was taken by the wind. It buffeted her, picking up in intensity as thick snow began to fall. It was fast, driven by the wind, and it hit her exposed legs and arms, freezing them so that she could hardly move. She struggled to carry on following, but the stranger was getting away.

He was taking Jessica away from her.

Her legs seemed to lengthen, causing her to stumble. Sadie looked down to see that she was grown again, and in her federal uniform. Now she could catch up.

"Jessica, I'm coming!" she screamed, pulling her gun.

But Jessica was fading, her edges becoming blurry, and Sadie screamed into the wind, knowing it was futile.

She couldn't save her.

The door knocked and Sadie sat straight up, her eyes flying open.

"Jessica?"

There was a pause, then Deputy Cooper's voice brought her out of her dream and into reality.

"We have some intel on the second body. The Sheriff told me to come and get you. I'll wait downstairs." Sadie heard her footsteps retreating down the hall. She jumped out of the bed and headed for the shower, the nightmare already retreating back into the shadows of her mind as the knowledge that there was work to do took over.

She quickly showered and threw on her clothes, plaited her hair back and grabbed her ski jacket, gloves and scarf, then made her way downstairs to meet the Deputy. She was torn between hoping the other woman hadn't heard her call out her sister's name and feeling pleasantly surprised that the Sheriff had insisted she be picked straight up. She hoped things were on the way to thawing between them after their poor start yesterday.

Logan Cooper seemed like a good, solid cop. One who cared and cared about the job. Sadie had been around enough corrupt cops in her time to appreciate the ones with some integrity. Making the right choice wasn't always easy – and she knew that better than anyone.

As she passed the kitchen the smell of burnt bacon and tobacco hit her. The sooner she got out of here and found a permanent place, the better. She had some house viewings on her agenda, but this case could throw her schedule off for days, if not longer.

That really depended on whether any more bodies showed up.

Deputy Cooper hovered by the front door, her mouth curled up in distaste.

"I would have thought a BAU expert could afford better than this," she said, not bothering to keep her voice down.

"It was the closest to the HQ," Sadie said. "So, what's up? Do we have an ID?"

"Jump in the snowcat and I'll fill you in," Jane told her, leading the way. As Sadie passed the Anchorage snow plough, she figured that she had better let Golightly know where it was and drop the keys back in to the office. No doubt her new boss would be chomping at the bit for a face-to-face update. The other woman rolled her eyes at the request but refrained from her usual baiting.

"We got a positive ID on the body from the lab," she said, and Sadie could hear the stress in her voice. This was bad.

"Go on."

"You were right, she is another prostitute and meth user. She's been busted for soliciting and possession but got away with community orders and rehab – which clearly didn't work. Another one of Montgomery's girls. Her name was Eva Aariak ."

Sadie's ears pricked up at the sound of her surname. "Aariak? Is she Inuit?"

"Half. And Verity Hagen is quarter. Looks like everyone forgot to mention that part; or maybe they didn't know. It's not immediately obvious. We located her parents too. They moved away a few years ago to Canada and apparently washed their hands of Verity after she failed rehab. The mother is half Native. They claim not to have spoken to her in years. We'll check it out, but I think they're a dead end."

Sadie sat back in her seat and whistled under her breath. She was less interested in Verity's parents than she was in the fact that both girls had dual ethnicities. Now she knew what had been niggling at her. Both Verity and Eva had slightly Native features and coloring, but not enough to be immediately apparent. Now she wondered if her hunch about the trapper had been right, or if it had simply been the ethnic connection that had been niggling at her.

"So, he – the perp, and assuming it's a he – has a type. Or it could be coincidence, if they were both working for Peter. I still say a john is an avenue we need to be looking down, but getting that information isn't going to be easy."

"We're going to meet Logan at Montgomery's now. At the moment he's our only link to both girls."

He was capable of killing them both, Sadie thought, thinking of the cruelty that she had always seen in him. She thought, too, of the way he had bullied and pestered the Native kids.

They swung by the FBI headquarters and Sadie went into the reception with the keys to the snow plough, wondering what Golightly would make of this newest development.

Golightly wasn't there, however, so she left the keys and the address of the motel with an awestruck young agent and went back outside. She was about to get back into the snowcat when a long, black vehicle stopped in the road just ahead of them, blocking Deputy Cooper from being able to pull out.

Sadie looked over at the number plate. GODS WORK.

A tall, dark-haired man in his fifties got out. He was well built, looking more like an ex-bodybuilder than a man of the church, and clean shaven and smartly dressed. His face was weathered but handsome, and he would have looked the epitome of the cool, modern preacher one saw so often these days, if it wasn't for his eyes.

They seemed to bore into Sadie as he approached, and she knew instantly what the gleam in them represented.

Fanaticism.

Behind her Deputy Cooper got out of the car, nodding warily at the man.

"Reverend Sutcliffe," she said in greeting. "Would you mind moving your car? You're blocking the road, and we're on official business. We don't have time to waste."

He nodded politely at the Deputy's words but he, kept his eyes fixed on Sadie, glancing down at her badge.

"Of course, Deputy, apologies," he said, his voice a deep drawl that Sadie imagined carried well on a Sunday. "And you must be the new Federal agent. I've heard that you are investigating these murders?"

Sadie felt herself freeze. The murders were not yet officially public knowledge, although she knew that the news would travel fast around here, and there was something about the way the man spoke about them that set her teeth on edge.

"What are you talking about, Reverend?" she said cautiously. The preacher rolled his eyes heavenward, and his voice took on a somber tone.

"The Native girls," he said, and his voice took on a disapproving tone. More than that, Sadie caught the tinge of disgust in his words.

"We haven't released details on the victims' ethnicity, Reverend," Deputy Cooper cut in.

"You know that they are heathens, most of them?" the preacher said, his eyes still on Sadie. She met his gaze coolly, not wanting him to know that he unnerved her. "The day will come," he said as though intoning a sermon, "when all of the heathens will be consumed in the pit of fire. Cleansed by the wrath of God. Heathens and heretics alike. You cannot save them, I'm afraid, Agent. They must save themselves by repenting and falling on His infinite mercy."

"I'm afraid we don't have time for this," the Deputy said, sounding exasperated. "We appreciate the impromptu sermon, I'm sure, but we really must be getting on."

He ignored her, taking a step forward. Sadie felt her hackles raise, an animal response to perceived threat in spite of the now friendly smile that the Reverend was giving her.

It made her think of a shark

"I would like to pray for you, Agent," he offered. "For you and your colleagues are dealing with more than just earthly evil. Those girls were flirting with the Devil. It has been foretold," he continued. "The heathens will be purified in both fire and ice. The deepest depths of Hell are cold, not hot. Did you know that? Most people don't."

Sadie's right hand twitched with the urge to go for her gun. Something about this guy just screamed predator. He certainly wasn't making her feel at all spiritual. "What do you know about the deaths?" she said, careful to avoid giving away any information that wasn't common knowledge.

"Yeah," the Deputy cut in, sounding almost as suspicious as Sadie. For once they were on the same page. "It seems that news sure does travel fast around here."

The preacher bowed his head. "God's Word is faster than any email," he said simply.

"That's interesting," Sadie said. "Does God's Word tell you anything else about them?"

He met her eyes again, and they shone with such fervor that Sadie would have suspected he had a fever if she had never come across religious fundamentalists before.

"You can mock me, Agent," he said with a long-suffering sigh, "but you would do well to take heed of Our Lord's teachings. Whoever killed those girls may be wicked, but sometimes wickedness serves its purpose. God does not allow sin and immorality to flourish for long. The heathens and their ways are a stain on this place." He gave an exaggerated shiver. "Prostitution, drugs, debauchery...such sins must be paid for."

Sadie made a mental note of his language. The concepts of stain and filth in relation to sin came up often, she knew. Was that why the killer had buried them in ice? Something that looked so pure and pristine, that cleansed absolutely? She shuddered and was about to continue to question him when the Deputy cut in, impatience straining her voice.

“How about you stay in your lane, Reverend, and let us do our job?” she said. “Because if you don’t hurry up and move that monstrosity of a car, I’m going to arrest you for obstruction.”

He didn’t look fazed, but simply nodded courteously at the policewoman and made his way back to his car. Sadie was glad to have him away from her; his proximity unnerved her. Before he slid his long legs back into the SUV, he addressed Sadie again.

“You mark my words,” he said ominously. “If the heathens do not change their ways, then the girls will not be the only ones to die, one way or another.”

“You watch over your flock,” Sadie said in a low voice that nevertheless carried across the street, “and I will watch over the ‘heathens’…and for anyone who tries to harm them.” She registered the threat in her own words and saw by the flicker of the preacher’s eyes that he had too. He drove away without another word, and Sadie watched the SUV disappear around the corner in front of them.

She realized the hairs on the back of her neck were standing on end.

CHAPTER THIRTEEN

What the hell was all that about? Sadie thought. The preacher gave her the creeps.

"We should bring him in for questioning, as soon as we've finished with Peter," she said. Deputy Cooper looked sideways at her.

"He's harmless enough," she protested. "Just a bit fire and brimstone, is all. You can't just show up in town and start arresting longstanding members of the community," she said.

Sadie was surprised at the Deputy's reluctance to consider the preacher as a suspect, even after his words about heathens. He sounded guilty as hell to her.

"He has too much information," she protested. "We've only just found out ourselves that the vics were both part Inuit."

The Deputy shrugged, clearly unimpressed with that particular detail in spite of the red flags it raised. Along with his clear hatred of unconverted Natives.

"After the shoe turned up at the Saloon," Jane pointed out, "the whole thing would have been all around Anchorage and the surrounding hinterlands. People don't have enough to do around here; gossip spreads fast."

"But not everyone would have known they were part Inuit," Sadie protested. "They weren't living with their people."

"Some must have," Jane argued back. "There's no reason to keep it secret. And they were hookers – they may even have used it as a calling card. Some guys specifically ask for that sort of thing. That's assuming this even has anything to do with their heritage. Verity was mostly white."

"I know. But we have to consider all angles. And believe me, ruling someone out just because they are religious is a big mistake."

Rather than arguing back, the Deputy actually looked interested in what Sadie had to say. "Have you seen that a lot? Ultra-religious perps?"

"I haven't personally brought in an actual preacher for anything," Sadie admitted. "But killers – especially if it does turn out that we're looking at a potential serial – are often motivated or inspired by religious motifs and themes. It's a bit of a stereotype, but unfortunately often a true one."

"Well, we'll see what Logan has to say," the policewoman said, her tone implying that the Sheriff would be as unimpressed with Sadie's theory as she was.

"Of course, now that we know they are of mixed ethnicity, there could be a purely racial motive," Sadie mused. The Deputy looked unsure.

"Racial? Come on now, I mean, this isn't the Fifties. Folks don't care about all that anymore, apart from maybe some of the old boys. It's all in the past."

Sadie shook her head at the Deputy's naiveté.

"Even when I was a kid, there was anti-Inuit feeling around here," she told her. "Maybe it's different in Juneau, but we're close to Inuit land here. Of course, it was all their land once. But there were definitely always tensions. Historically, we've treated the Inuit people terribly, and they're still feeling the effects."

The Deputy shook her head stubbornly, her eyes fixed on the road ahead as they drove out of Anchorage. Although the snowfall had eased it lay thicker and heavier on the ground than it had the day before. Sadie hoped the weather wouldn't get so bad that their investigations were cut short.

"Yeah, but that's historically. History, as in, in the past. Most people have moved on from all that, surely?" The other woman looked deeply uncomfortable with the whole topic. "We have equality now."

"Well, in law and on paper, sure," Sadie said, starting to feel exasperated, "but not everyone starts from a level playing field. Natives, on average, are way more likely to live in poverty, struggle to get decent employment...and Native girls and women go missing at serious levels. Add that to the fact that our victims were sex workers as well as minority ethnic...I'm not saying we put it front and center, but we need to bear the possibility in mind while we're investigating. So far, it feels like we're missing something about these murders, and the racial angle could be it."

"I don't know," the Deputy said, although her tone had softened somewhat, as though she might actually be considering Sadie's hypothesis. "I know this place; they're good people."

"Some are, some aren't," Sadie said. "I grew up here, remember?"

Sadie stared out of the window as she recalled her schooldays. She had been an introverted child, more so after her mother died of cancer and her father turned to the bottle, and she'd had to look out for her and Jessica.

Until Matthew had taken a shine to her, and her status as his girlfriend had propelled her to the edges of the popular crowd, her best friend throughout high school had been an Inuit girl called Mona, whose parents had wanted her to get the benefit of an American education. Sadie remembered the taunts that Mona had endured on the playground and the harassment at high school, including from the boys who seemed to simultaneously fetishize her and despise her. The teachers had turned a blind eye.

In fact, a few of the teachers had been just as bad, assuming Mona was less intelligent, or singling her out for bad behavior when other kids got away with far worse. Or just flat out ignoring her.

Mona had rolled her eyes at all of it, kept her head down and worked hard; but one night when they were doing homework together, she had cried to Sadie about it, and Sadie had never forgotten. She wondered where Mona was now.

"There were Native kids at school," was all Sadie revealed to the other woman. "I saw the crap that some of them put up with, and the teachers, for the most part, let it slide. And the boys always hassled the Native girls...it's that whole 'exotic' nonsense. I don't believe that will all have magically gone away. And as far as our killer is concerned, we need to consider all possible motivations."

The Deputy didn't answer her, and they drove on in silence, both wrapped up in their own thoughts.

*

Sadie jumped out of the snowcat outside Montgomery's place. The sky was rapidly darkening and the clouds that were rolling in were a heavy cobalt, weighted with the threat of more snow. The wind was picking up, snatching tendrils of Sadie's hair out of her plait from under her hood and whipping them around her face. There was a bite in the wind, blowing straight down from the Arctic.

The Sheriff was waiting for them, stamping his feet against the cold. As Sadie approached, he wasted no time on pleasantries.

"I take it Jane filled you in on the girls?"

"Yes," Sadie said, deciding to save her theories until later, after they had questioned Peter Montgomery. If he answered the door, that was. Sadie wasn't so sure about the logic of coming mob handed like this; it didn't need three of them to question him. If Montgomery had any sense, he would have heard the vehicles pulling up and crept out of the back.

Cooper pounded loudly at the door of the old house, but there was no answer and no sign of life from within.

"Montgomery! Open up!" the Deputy hollered.

"Perhaps he saw us coming and went out the back way," Sadie suggested.

She walked around the back of the house to see if there was any sign of him leaving that way. The back door was boarded up, but she saw a shed down the bottom of a small hill at the back of the house, and it pricked her interest.

As she jogged towards it, she saw that it had no windows, and then caught a faint scent that she recognized and that stopped her in her tracks. She knew exactly what the outhouse was being used for.

Sadie unclasped the holster to her gun and raised her radio to her mouth.

"Sheriff," she whispered into it, "Come round the back…quietly."

Cooper and his sister emerged from around the side of the house and walked towards her. There was a frown on Cooper's face as he approached, looking around him.

"Do you think he's in there?" he asked, nodding towards the outhouse.

Sadie nodded. "Smell anything?" she asked.

He sniffed the air. The faint scent of rotten eggs mixed with cat urine drifted towards them.

"Meth," he said, shaking his head. "The son of a bitch." He stalked towards the shed, drawing his own gun and motioning for them to get in behind him. Sadie glanced at the Deputy.

"Have you taken down a meth operation before?" Sadie asked her. Jane Cooper shook her head, looking more excited than nervous.

"Don't shoot anything or anyone unless it is completely unavoidable," Sadie advised her. "Or the whole outhouse could explode. Cooking meth is a highly flammable process."

"Idiots," the Deputy murmured.

"For once, we agree completely," Sadie told her as they followed Cooper. The Deputy gave her a quick grin.

Wasting no time, the Sheriff kicked in the door to the outhouse, yelling for whoever was inside to get their hands up. Sadie came in behind him, seeing Peter standing behind a makeshift lab with his hands in the air and an expression of resignation on his face. He wasn't getting out of this one in a hurry.

Next to him was a young woman with stringy blonde hair, who Sadie would bet was barely more than eighteen. She looked terrified, and the hands she held in the air were visibly trembling. Sadie shot a look of disgust at Peter, wondering if he was pimping this girl out too, even though she was barely more than a child.

"What's your name?" she said to the girl as the Deputy arrested and cuffed her, leaving Cooper to deal with Montgomery.

"Gemma," the girl said in a small voice. There were telltale scabs on her lips.

"How old are you, Gemma?"

The girl hesitated, and then mumbled, "Seventeen." Sadie wondered if the Sheriff would turn another blind eye if she broke Peter Montgomery's nose too.

"Your parents know you're here? Anyone we can call?" she asked in a softer tone. The girl shook her head, a touch of defiance showing through her obvious fear.

"Ain't seen my parents in years. I was fostered. They weren't no good either. Peter looks after me."

I bet he does, Sadie thought. She watched as the Deputy hauled the girl out of the shed. Something about the teenager tugged at Sadie's heartstrings. If she hadn't been set on joining the FBI, perhaps in a displaced attempt to avenge her sister's death, who was to say that wouldn't have been her? With a dead mother, a drowned sister and an alcoholic father that would rather beat her than hug her, it would have been all too easy to go down the wrong path.

There but for the grace of God go I.

The phrase made her think of Reverend Sutcliffe, and she made a mental note to talk to Cooper about him, too. She wasn't convinced that Peter Montgomery was their killer, even if, so far, it pointed in his direction.

As she followed the Coopers, being careful not to disturb anything, something on a side shelf caught her eye.

A pink cosmetics bag, stained with what looked like some kind of shimmery eyeshadow, and with a pom-pom that had seen better days.

Two large, silver initials were printed on the front, and Sadie felt her stomach twist as she saw them.

E.A.

Eva Aariak.

CHAPTER FOURTEEN

There were two small interview rooms at the station. They left a red-faced and angry Peter in one, demanding a lawyer, while the Sheriff and Sadie went to interview Gemma, leaving Deputy Cooper to co-ordinate the dismantling of the makeshift meth lab.

Sitting opposite Gemma, Sadie felt a similar rush of compassion for her to the one she had experienced in the lab. Under the flickering lights of the interview room, which highlighted her freckles and the crop of acne on her chin, the girl looked even younger.

"I'm not telling you nothing," Gemma announced, raising her chin. "This is entrapment."

Cooper grinned at her, not unkindly.

"I'm afraid," he said in a firm voice as though he was chiding a schoolgirl – which really, she was – "we've got you dead to rights, Gemma. You were literally cooking up a batch of meth right in front of us. That's serious time, even for a minor. There's a good chance they'll lock you up with the adults, I mean you're nearly eighteen, right? You can look after yourself, isn't that what you told us on the way here?"

Gemma shrank back into her chair, obviously terrified in spite of her attempts at defiance, but didn't answer. Sadie leaned over the table towards her.

"Gemma," she said in a gentle voice, "if Peter was coercing you, to help him with the drugs, or was violent to you in any way…" She left the question hanging. Gemma's eyes flickered and she looked away, and under the strip light there was a faint suggestion of an old bruise around her eye. Sadie clenched her jaw and exhaled slowly.

But the girl's loyalty – or fear – wasn't going to let her betray Peter so easily. She shook her head vehemently.

"Peter is good to me," she insisted. "He looks after me."

"Bit of a father figure, is he?" Cooper said. Gemma glared at him. "What would you know?" she all but spat the words out, a fine mist of spittle landing on the table between them. "I'm over the age of consent. You can't do nothing."

"Is he pimping you out?" Cooper responded. Gemma looked shocked and immediately clammed up, but Sadie saw her expression flood with shame and guessed that Cooper was right.

"Peter won't protect you, Gemma," she said, using the same soothing sort of tone she might use on an injured animal. "If he could pin this on you, he would, believe me. We go back a long way. Luckily, he's not wriggling out of the meth charges, whether you give us anything or not. He will know that. But we can help you."

Gemma looked suspicious but interested. "Help me how?"

Sadie glanced at Cooper, who gave her a small, almost imperceptible nod, authorizing her to bargain with the girl. Technically, she didn't need his authorization, but she knew he would appreciate the gesture, and they needed to work together if they were going to crack this.

"Get you in a rehab program, or, if the Sheriff here is right – and you don't necessarily have to disclose this to us, we can get a social worker in here – a program for exploited girls. There will be conditions, but we can keep you out of jail and help you turn things around. You deserve better than the life Peter is offering you, Gemma. Do you want to end up like Verity and Eva?"

There was no mistaking the girl's reaction. She sat back in her chair as though she had been shot.

"Eva? She's dead too?"

Sadie searched the girl's face. Her reaction was immediate and authentic; she hadn't known Eva was dead. The news report that morning had stated only that another body had been found, no mention of her identity, or of the shoe.

Sadie nodded sadly.

"Yep. Afraid so. Such a waste of life."

"Peter had nothing to do with it," Gemma insisted. "I don't know why you questioned him yesterday. It's harassment, he said so. Verity took off weeks ago. They were jealous of me, because I'm younger, see?" She said the last part proudly and it made Sadie wince as she picked up the implication. Younger, as in more popular with the johns.

"And what about Eva?" Cooper cut in, sounding impatient. "We found her bag in the outhouse, so we know that she was involved somewhere along the line. It's not looking good for Peter at all. Two of his girls turn up dead in the space of two days? If you withhold any information from us, Gemma, you could be charged as an accessory."

"Accessory?" the girl all but whimpered.

“To murder,” Cooper clarified. Gemma looked as though she was about to burst into tears.

“Peter didn’t kill them, I know he didn’t,” she said. “Why would he?”

“They set up on their own, didn’t they, after Peter got rid of them?” Sadie asked. “We know they were prostituting, Gemma. Eva has – had - form. Perhaps he was worried they would cut into his profits, that they weren’t so used up after all.”

Gemma frowned and Sadie could see that she didn’t understand. The story that Matthew had given them wasn’t one that resonated with her.

“Used up? Peter didn’t…he didn’t get rid of them. They left. Peter was angry, really angry, but he wouldn’t kill them.” For the first time, she didn’t sound so sure, but was looking at Sadie as though she wanted the older woman to reassure her.

Sadie and Cooper stayed silent, watching Gemma as she played things over in her own mind.

“Can you really keep me out of prison?” she asked eventually.

“We can do our best,” Sadie told her. “The more you cooperate, the better.”

“I don’t know what I can tell you,” the girl protested, obviously on the verge of tears. “You know about the meth. About the…escorting. I don’t know what happened to Verity and Eva, but it can’t have been Peter.”

“It can’t, or you don’t want it to be?” Cooper said. Gemma looked at the floor.

“He promised me that he would look after me,” she whispered.

“He can’t look after you from prison, Gemma, and he’s going there regardless. Anything you know about Eva and Verity could help us, anything at all,” Sadie urged.

Gemma sighed, leaning back in her chair and staring up at the ceiling as she spoke.

“It was weeks ago,” she said. “Eva started complaining that they needed more money. Her and Verity were friends, I think because they were both mixed, you know? Peter used to call them ‘half-breeds’ when he was mad or high. But the johns liked it, so he wouldn’t have got rid of them.”

“Peter sounds like a real stand-up guy,” Cooper interrupted with a sarcastic drawl. Sadie shot him a look, warning him to shut up. They didn’t want to alienate Gemma just as she was opening up.

The girl continued, ignoring Cooper's comment. "He used to pay them in meth, mostly, even for helping out in the lab. Eva got mad and said he should be cutting them in on the profits. Verity agreed; she always agreed with Eva, all the time, and said she wasn't going to work until he sorted them out. Peter …hit her."

"He hit her?"

"Yeah, just a slap, but then Eva pulled a knife on him, and he stopped. She said they were leaving to set up on their own, that they would set up their own lab, and they wouldn't need him. Peter laughed at her and let them go. That's it. I don't know anything else."

Sadie nodded slowly. "Thank you, Gemma. That's really helpful, honestly. The only thing is…you can't be sure he didn't kill them, can you? I mean, he hit Verity and Eva threatened him with a knife. I can't see him taking that lying down, can you? He would lose face, surely?"

Gemma shook her head. "He was mad, but he said he didn't care because they would never make it on their own. They didn't know the first thing about cooking meth until they met him. He said being hookers were all they were good for. But…" she clammed up, her eyes darting between the Sheriff and Sadie.

"But what, Gemma?" Sadie asked quietly.

"Then we heard they had hooked up with some guy, that they were staying at his place and all going into business together. At first, he was mad, but then he found out who it was, and he laughed and said he was another meth head loser, and they would never get anywhere. He said it wasn't even worth his time to worry about."

"Do you know the other guy's name?"

"No. But maybe he killed them."

"Any dodgy johns that you know of?" Sadie asked, changing tack. "You said the women used their ethnicity as a way to attract them; do you remember either of them talking about a john bothering them?"

Gemma shook her head. "No, that's all I know." She seemed to sag in her chair like a deflated balloon. Sadie and Cooper exchanged glances.

"Okay, Gemma," Cooper said, "I'm going to get a lawyer and a social worker in to talk to you about the meth, and they can start the ball rolling in trying to get you into a program. It might take a while for anyone to get here; the weather forecast is dire. That means time in the cells. We'll try and make you as comfortable as possible. If you think of anything else that could be useful…."

Gemma looked terrified again, and Sadie guessed it wasn't just about the cells so much as being left here for possibly days without any drugs. She would be coming down at some point, and craving, and it wouldn't be pretty.

They left her staring at the ceiling waiting for a State Trooper to come in and take her down to the cells and headed towards Peter's room.

"Do you think it was him?" Cooper asked quietly. Sadie sighed.

"Honestly? No, I don't, but if we look at the evidence…he knew both girls and has a motive. It certainly needs pursuing."

"Either way, he will be locked up for a long time," Cooper said, a look of disgust on his face. "What he's been doing to those girls…this one is barely more than a child."

"I know," Sadie said in a soft voice, thinking about the girl. She hoped that this would be a turning point for Gemma, that the girl would beat the statistics and turn her life around.

And stay away from men like Peter Montgomery.

Peter was, like Gemma, cuffed to the table, but unlike the girl he looked more bored than frightened. It had to be bravado. Montgomery might fancy himself as a hotshot drug dealer, but Sadie suspected that he would last all of two minutes in prison.

As they sat down opposite him, he curled his lip in a sneer.

"What do you two want? I'm not saying anything without a lawyer."

"It's not about the lab," Cooper said in a friendly manner, passing him a roll-up over the table. Peter looked surprised then grabbed at it, leaning towards Cooper for a light.

"Then what?"

"While you're here, we have a few questions about Verity Hagen." Cooper didn't mention Eva. Peter rolled his eyes as he took a long drag on the tobacco joint.

"That again? I told you, I don't know anything. And I'm not answering any questions about her either. You're trying to entrap me."

"We're investigating a murder, Peter," Cooper said. It was the first time that Sadie had heard the Sheriff use the man's first name. "We just need all the background information we can get, that's all."

Peter took another long drag, seeming to enjoy making them wait. "I don't know why you're bothering," he said. "She was a piece of shit anyway."

“Was Eva Aariak a piece of shit as well?” Sadie snapped. Peter blinked at her, looking confused.

“Eva? What’s she got to do with it?”

“She’s dead,” Sadie said flatly, remembering the woman’s lifeless body being hauled out of the lake near the gorge. “Murdered. Like Verity.”

Peter’s eyes went wide with what seemed like genuine shock. He ignored Sadie and looked at Cooper instead.

“Look, I had nothing to do with this,” he said. “I can’t tell you anything. I’m in enough trouble…if I knew anything I would tell you.”

Cooper didn’t answer, leaving Sadie to come in again. Without discussing it they had switched roles from Gemma’s interview, and this time she wasn’t the good cop, which was just fine by her. They seemed to naturally work well together, a nice contrast from the hostility and mistrust from the day before.

Maybe she could get on with Logan Cooper after all.

“We found Eva’s cosmetics bag in your shed,” she said. “So, we know she was helping you run your little operation. And she was a hooker like Verity. So, you were pimping her too. What happened? Did you fall out with Eva too and decide to get rid of them both?”

“Whoa!” Peter protested. He looked at Cooper for help. “I knew that you were trying to pin this on me. What did that little bitch tell you?”

“Gemma? She was very loyal to you Peter – more than you deserve.” Sadie gave him a mirthless smile. “You know she’s a minor, right? You could be looking at a sex trafficking charge here. Do you know what they do to child traffickers in prison?”

Peter looked like he wanted to hit her, and Sadie half wished that he would. She would love a chance to get her hands on him.

“The thing is, Peter,” Cooper came in, sounding almost sorrowful, “it really isn’t looking good for you at all. If nothing else, you will do a long stretch for the meth. No lawyer can get you out of that. If you have any information on Eva and Verity – anything at all – it could really help. We could say you cooperated. It might help shave off a few years.”

“Unless you killed them,” Sadie added. “In which case you’re looking at two life sentences. The polar caps will have melted before you get out.”

Peter stared hard at her, and Sadie met his gaze coolly. Peter dropped his eyes first, knowing when he was beaten.

"Ask your ex-boyfriend about that," he said finally. "Eva went to stay there too. They were talking some shit about setting up their own lab…as far as I know it didn't happen. Matthew was still buying off me."

"Why didn't you mention Eva when we asked you about Verity?"

Peter shrugged. "Why would I? The less people know I lost two of my girls, the better."

"See, that's bothering me, Peter," Cooper said, dropping the jovial tone. "You were just going to let them walk away? What kind of pimp is that?"

Peter went red. "They weren't going to get anywhere," he snapped. "I warned people not to buy off them if they did. I warned Matthew. It was enough. If they had crossed me again…" he trailed off, perhaps realizing that making threats against two recently murdered girls was not a good look.

"You would what?" Sadie quipped. "Kill them?"

Peter stuck his middle finger up at her.

"I'm not saying anything else without a lawyer. This is harassment."

"So, you keep saying," Cooper said with a yawn. He stood up, and Sadie followed. They left Peter staring after them without another word.

In the corridor outside, they paused to take stock. Sadie ran a hand over her hair, patting her braid into place. She looked out of the window to see the snow had started up again.

"It wasn't him," she said. "I know he's probably one of our chief suspects right now, but I don't think it's him."

"Neither do I, truth be told," Cooper agreed. "What about Matthew Collins? Your first instinct was that it was him, right?"

"I think he might be capable of it," she said cautiously, "and is at least as likely to be the culprit as Peter."

"But?"

Sadie hesitated for a moment. "I still think the race angle is key here. It's just a hunch, nothing more, but I think we should keep it in mind."

Cooper didn't look convinced. "It could just be coincidence. They were friends. Cooking meth together, soliciting together. They had a lot more in common than just some shared DNA. I don't see any evidence for it being relevant. But sure, let's keep it in mind."

Sadie knew that he was humoring her but decided to let it go for now. She wasn't looking forward to questioning Matthew Collins, especially with Cooper there. She felt uncomfortable, knowing that Cooper knew her history with Matthew, and even more so since the Deputy's jibes about her sister. More than that, she had a feeling that her old flame would be a lot more forthcoming if it was just her.

"I want to question Matthew alone," she said.

"What? No, way."

"We will get more out of him if it's just me," Sadie insisted. "You saw what he was like yesterday. He's strung out, paranoid, emotional, and on a hair trigger. I can get through to him."

Cooper tipped his head to one side, considering. Then he gave a heavy sigh.

"All right. You can take the snowcat. You're a good detective. And I have a whole load of paperwork to do for Montgomery and the girl. But you stay in touch and radio immediately if he seems hostile, all right? Your history could go against you; he could feel betrayed, or resentful, and it might make him even more volatile. But your judgment has been sound so far. Just be careful; I don't need Golightly on my case for getting his new agent hurt."

Sadie was already on her way out of the door.

She hoped that she wasn't on her way to arrest her ex-boyfriend for a double homicide.

CHAPTER FIFTEEN

Sadie pounded on the door of Matthew's rundown bungalow, hoping that he was at home, and actually lucid enough to be of any use. She heard the sound of shuffling coming from inside.

"Who is it?" he called, and she heard the note of paranoia in his voice.

"Special Agent Price," Sadie said automatically, then added in a softer voice. "It's Sadie, Matthew. I just wanted to have a quick chat. I don't have Sheriff Cooper with me."

"Wait there. I'll be one minute," Matthew mumbled through the door. She heard him moving around inside and guessed that he was hiding his meth, possibly even flushing it. That wouldn't make him happy.

When he opened the door, he looked even paler and more underweight than he had the day before, but Sadie was relieved to see that his pupils were a relatively normal size, and he didn't seem too out of it.

"What do you want, Sadie?" he asked. "I'm pretty busy."

"I said we would be back with a few more questions," Sadie said lightly. "Today seemed as good a time as any."

"Not for me, it isn't." Matthew went to shut the door, only to find that Sadie had wedged her foot firmly between it and the wooden frame.

"Eva is dead too," she said quietly, looking him straight in the eye. "Why didn't you tell us that she was staying here with Verity?"

Matthew looked shocked and scared but not, Sadie noted, particularly surprised. Of course, the news about Eva had no doubt travelled fast too.

"She wasn't…not really. Eva does her own thing. She disappears a lot."

"Can I come in, Matthew?" Sadie asked, softening her voice. "It's pretty wild out here." As she spoke, the wind howled fiercely, and a bin lid rattled loudly down the street behind her. As Golightly had predicted, the weather was worsening fast.

Matthew still looked unsure, but he stepped aside to let Sadie in. She stepped past him into the hall, wrinkling her nose against the smell of unwashed laundry and general dirt. Matthew motioned for her to go into the front room.

"Sit down," he offered. Sadie gingerly perched on the edge of the filthy looking armchair while Matthew sat on the edge of the table, looking forlorn. She tried not to feel too much sympathy for him, but it was difficult not to remember what he had once meant to her, before he had become this twitching shell of a man. Right now, staring down at his hands, he looked harmless, but Sadie remembered the simmering violence that she had seen in him the day before, and she kept her hand close to her holster. Although her instincts told her otherwise, she knew that he was still every inch a suspect in this case.

"I didn't kill them," he blurted out, as though reading her mind.

"No one is accusing you of killing anyone," Sadie said, leaving the 'yet' hanging in the air between them. Matthew shifted uncomfortably on the table, still staring at his hands. His fingers were covered in the same burn marks that she had spotted on the hands of Eva and Verity, and for a moment she felt only pity.

"But it does seem odd that you didn't mention Eva yesterday," Sadie went on. "Weren't you concerned that she was missing as well? Didn't it occur to you that she might have met the same fate? If we had known she was missing too, we could have looked for her." Although they were fairly sure the girls had been killed around the same time, she didn't need to tell Matthew that. Playing on any emotions he had left might encourage him to open up and give her something useful.

Instead, Matthew looked angry and lifted his eyes to her for the first time. "I'm not taking the blame for this," he snapped. "They both did their own thing, especially Eva. They were always disappearing. I'm not the only one they smoked meth with," he said, sounding faintly disgusted. Sadie raised an eyebrow.

"You sound annoyed about that?"

"They used me," Matthew told her, his expression begging for understanding. "I said they could stay here, that I would help them out, I let them bring tricks back here, and they just come and go like it's a hotel."

Sadie nodded, her face carefully neutral. Matthew continued, getting into his story and seeming unaware that he was potentially incriminating himself.

"Were you sleeping with Eva too?" she asked. Matthew looked shamefaced.

"No…there was one time…they offered me a threesome in place of rent."

"And you went along with that?"

Matthew shrugged. "Sure. What man wouldn't?" He grinned at her and she saw that some of his teeth were missing. She refrained from telling him what she truly thought – that no decent man would behave as he had, taking advantage of clearly vulnerable women – and asked instead, "Did it cause problems? Did Verity get jealous, maybe?"

He shook his head, looking almost smug. Sadie wondered if he seriously expected her to be impressed with his revelation, as though it was proof of his innate charm.

"Nah, man," he said. "It was cool."

He winked at her.

Sadie felt nauseous and decided to change track.

"We heard that when the girls left Peter, it was their intention to start cooking up and selling the meth themselves. Were you a part of that, Matthew? Is that why they were staying here?" She looked around, peering out into the hall. "This place isn't a bad size. Do you have an outhouse?"

Matthew flinched visibly, and there was guilt written all over his face. "I don't know what you're talking about," he protested, his eyes flickering from side to side. "Peter told you that, didn't he? He's trying to frame me. It was him; I'm telling you, you should be questioning him, not me."

So, the news hadn't yet spread about the raid on Peter's place. Sadie sighed and gave Matthew what she hoped was a sympathetic smile. Part of her wanted to empathize with him, to find some trace of the boy she had known, but the more she heard about his dealings with the victims, the harder that was.

"Look, Matty," she said, using the name that she had used for him when they were kids, "It's better you tell me the truth now, while it's just me, than wait for the Sheriff to haul you in. I'm sure you know that this doesn't look good. We already know that you were using math with the girls, sleeping with them, and taking prostitution money from them for rent…not to mention allowing it to go on here. That's a brothel-keeping charge, and if we add drug dealing on top of that…."

Matthew looked panicked, shaking his head from side to side. "That's not fair!" he gabbled. "I've answered your questions!"

"Then answer this one," Sadie said, a note of steel creeping into her voice, "Were you cooking meth with them?"

Two spots of color appeared on Matthew's gaunt cheeks, and he hung his head.

"We were supposed to," he admitted, "But it didn't really get off the ground. We were smoking too much…and then my other source dried up and I had to go back to Peter for the gear." He swallowed, his face flaming further, and Sadie guessed it must have been an acute humiliation to go crawling back to his old dealer after hooking up with Eva and Verity.

"And then what happened? Did Peter get wind of your plans?"

"He knew. Eva had taunted him before they left," he said, corroborating Peter's story. "He threatened me, said if I tried to deal on his patch, he would knife me and them."

"You believed him," Sadie said, a statement rather than a question. She could see the fear in Matthew's face. He nodded, looking embarrassed again.

"He's a nasty bastard," he said. "That's why, if anyone killed them, it's probably him."

"But then why wouldn't he kill them earlier," she replied, voicing her own thoughts. "Why bother now? You and the girls had shown him that you were no threat to him."

Matthew shrugged.

"Did either of them have any more run-ins with Peter?" Sadie asked.

"Not that I know of."

Sadie felt frustrated. So far, they were finding nothing but dead ends. Any motive Peter had was crumbling, and other than Matthew's proximity to the girls, there was nothing concrete to implicate him, either. As it stood, they had no other leads.

She was determined not to let any more girls suffer the same fate as her sister. To be washed up from a frozen lake, their killer never caught. To be forgotten by all except by those that loved them.

Again, Matthew seemed to almost read her mind.

"This must be tough for you, Sades," he said, and his use of his old name for her made her jump. "It's too much like Jessica, isn't it?"

Sadie blinked at him, wondering how to respond. Grief washed over her.

"I've never forgotten about it either, you know," he said, and now he was sympathizing with her, and she sensed that it was genuine, or as much as he was capable of these days. "I know what it did to you, losing her like that. And your dad. No one sees him now, you know. He's a complete recluse."

Sadie bit her lip at the mention of her father. Always a cold, occasionally violent man, he had made no secret of his disgust that he had been left with Sadie and that he would have preferred it if it had been her in that lake, not Jessica.

"Jessica was so beautiful," Matthew went on. "All the boys had crushes on her, you know. Except me, of course," he said hastily. "I was always stuck on you."

I remember," Sadie said quietly, finding it difficult not to be dragged back into memories of their past. "You were there for me after she died, when I was a total mess. I'm sorry that I just skipped town on you."

"I always knew you would," he said sadly. "You're better than this place. I don't know why you came back, to be honest."

"Closure, maybe," she said. *And to bring Jessica's killer to justice, if I can,* she continued in her mind. Matthew looked thoughtful for a moment, then he leaned forward, lowering his voice conspiratorially.

"Listen, Sades, do you think it could all be connected? Jessica's murder, I mean, and Verity and Eva's?"

Sadie's mouth went dry. "There's no reason to think so," she said quickly, deciding it was time to cut off the reminiscing. "We need to focus on Verity and Eva."

"Yes, but what if it's the same guy?" Matthew insisted. "Peter had a crush on Jessica, you know," he declared, sitting back triumphantly. Sadie eyed him suspiciously, wondering if that was even true or if he was just trying to shift the blame onto the other man again. Sadie didn't remember Peter ever hassling Jessica – not more than he did anyone else, anyway.

She changed the subject abruptly, even though part of her wanted to question him about Jessica more. She knew that the man he was now couldn't be trusted. Still, it was a possibility that she filed away in her mind to ruminate on later.

"Yesterday, we asked you about the girls' johns," she said. "Did any come to mind? Anyone that hung around a lot, got nasty or that the girls said seemed creepy?"

Matthew looked disappointed that she hadn't picked up his bait, but wisely decided not to push it. He made a show of thinking hard, cocking his head to one side. His neck was so skinny it looked as though it might snap at any moment.

"No," he said eventually. "They worked all over, not just in Anchorage. I know Eva had regulars that she stayed out of town with, but she didn't tell me anything about them. Sometimes she visited her mom too. She's an Inuit, you know."

"I know," Sadie said, her brow creasing. Her hunch that the girls' ethnicity was important hadn't gone anywhere. Of course, that made it a lot less likely that this was in any way connected to Jessica's murder, but Sadie knew that she couldn't let her desire to find justice for her sister obscure her own instincts on this case.

"Was that important to the girls?" she asked. "Their Inuit heritage?"

Matthew nodded. "Yeah. More so to Eva than to Verity, but Verity tended to go along with whatever Eva did. She was the more headstrong, definitely. In fact, that's why I didn't take much notice that I hadn't seen them for days. If they weren't out working, I figured they were preparing for that feast they have, the midwinter one. I don't know how to say it."

"Quviasukvik," Sadie said thoughtfully. It was the Inuit winter feast, celebrating their New Year, a blend of Christmas influences with Inuit pre-Christian beliefs that celebrated the sun at the time of year when it was the darkest – a widespread motif in indigenous and pagan cultures. It was a time of joy and feasting, and so it would have been natural for Matthew to assume that Eva at least had gone to spend this time of year with family.

"Do you know much about Eva's relationship with her mother?"

Matthew shook his head. "No. They still spoke, but she didn't talk about her much. I know she hated her dad, but I don't know why. I don't think he's Inuit. Verity's parents moved away. She phoned them when she wanted money," he said matter-of-factly. "She wasn't going home for Christmas. I thought we might spend it together," he said, looking sorry for himself again. "At least, if she wasn't celebrating the Inuit one with Eva."

Sadie felt a thought tugging at her, trying to get her attention. "Doesn't Anchorage council put on something for Quviasukvik?" she asked. "For diversity?"

"They do something, at the schools, but it's not as popular as it used to be. A lot of the more religious folk complain, especially since we've had that new Baptist preacher. He's a proper hellfire sort."

Sadie nodded and stood up. "I know. We've met," she said shortly, her head whirring. Reverend Sutcliffe clearly detested the Inuit, seeing them as 'heathens.' Could the impending Quviasukvik celebrations have wound him up to fever pitch? "Thank you, Matthew, you've been really helpful."

He stood up with her, looking disappointed.

"It was nice to see you, Sades," he said. "Why don't you stay for a bit? We could spend some time together." He winked at her again, which was obviously intended to look flirtatious but only struck Sadie as grotesque. She shook her head.

"Please?" he begged, looking suddenly desperate. "I'm on my own now that Verity and Eva have.... gone," he said. His dirty, burnt fingers brushed her arm, and Sadie had to fight not to recoil from his touch, instead carefully stepping away from him.

"It's hardly appropriate. I'm in the middle of a murder investigation," she reminded him.

"I just thought…for old time's sake…" Matthew mumbled. Sadie shook her head.

"What happened to you, Matthew?" she asked. "How did you end up like this?"

Matthew's face twisted as though he might cry, but then his face set into an angry expression, reminding Sadie of the way he had turned on her and the Sheriff yesterday. "We can't all skip town and get hotshot careers with the FBI," he said bitterly. "There's nothing here, just dead-end jobs and snow. I wanted to enjoy myself. Things just got out of hand. I'll get back on my feet; I've got plans," he assured her.

"Right. Well, let me know if you think of anything else," Sadie said. "I'll see myself out." She turned to leave, glad to get away from him but also sad to leave him in the state he was so clearly in. But she knew that she couldn't help him now; only he could do that.

He followed her to the front door anyway, his face mournful. His mercurial moods unnerved her, even as she knew they were typical of someone taking meth to the degree he clearly was. She remembered him as a mild-mannered, even-tempered boy, but she wondered now if the darker tendencies had always been there, and she just hadn't noticed.

"Should I have your number, in case I think of anything else?" he said as she walked to the vehicle, desperation in his voice. Sadie smiled tightly at him over her shoulder.

"You can call the Sheriff," she said. "Anything that you think might be helpful, don't hesitate," she added, not wanting to discourage him from passing information on. He nodded glumly.

As she slid into the snowcat, started the engine and pulled away, she was vaguely aware of him watching her go. But Sadie already had other things on her mind. Matthew's mention of the Inuit winter festival had made her think. Perhaps it wasn't the girls' ethnicity that was the issue here, but their religious customs.

She was going to see the heathen-hating preacher.

CHAPTER SIXTEEN

Sadie walked into Anchorage Baptist church, stamping the snow off her boots. Driving here had been hard going, and she had turned the radio on to find the blizzard warnings on high alert. She hoped the weather wouldn't get so bad that it pushed them off the case. The trail was already starting to go cold and having to miss any days now could be crucial.

The small church was empty, apart from a figure kneeling in front of the altar. The church was a simple, stone building, with a huge wooden cross hanging at the back of the communion table. Candles flickered on either side of it, casting an eerie light over the church's interior.

As Sadie approached, her boots were loud on the stone floor and the figure looked around and stood up, a suspicious look on his face as he saw Sadie approaching.

"Agent, a pleasure to see you again," the Reverend said drily, his tone making it clear that it was anything but. Sadie inclined her head in greeting.

"I'm sorry to interrupt your prayers," she said politely.

He smiled, but there was no warmth in it, only a strange gleam in his eyes.

"I was praying for the souls of those in this place that have yet to find our Lord," he said, his eyes burning into hers. "Have you found Him, Agent…Price, is it?"

Sadie glanced up at the cross. Maybe once, as a child, she had dared to hope that there was something more than human out there, something that cared for her in a way her own father never could, but Jessica's death had wrenched that hope away from her.

"Thank you for your concern, Reverend, but I'm not here about my soul. I wanted to ask you a few questions."

"About those murdered heathens?" Sutcliffe didn't look at all alarmed, instead he crossed his arms with a pompous expression. "You can ask away, Agent. I can assure you that I have nothing to hide."

Sadie tipped her head to one side, considering. "What makes you think I'm here to ask about the bodies?"

A smile played around his lips, almost mocking, and Sadie realized that this man really wasn't scared at all. Because he was innocent, she wondered, or because he was so convinced by his own bullshit that he thought his God would protect him no matter what? Some killers, she knew, almost perversely wanted to be found.

"Why else are you here if not for the sake of your soul? Or is there some other crime you would like to accuse me of? Many a follower of our Lord is persecuted unjustly, but we shall receive our reward in the times to come."

Sadie fought not to roll her eyes.

"I'm not accusing you. Unless you have something that you would like to confess?"

He just laughed, a condescending tone that grated on Sadie's ears. For a moment, she wondered why she had bothered to come here. This man would likely tell her nothing even if there was anything to tell.

"So come, Agent," he said. "What would you like to know? I can assure you I am always either here, with my flock, or with my devoted wife."

If only they had a better idea of time of death, it would be worth asking for an alibi. As it was, Sadie simply stared up at the altar, noticing the small Nativity scene that stood off to one side.

"It must make you mad, seeing the 'heathens' celebrate their own customs at this time of year," she said, and watched the preacher's face screw up into the mask of hatred that she had seen in the street that morning. The change was so instantaneous it was as though a switch had been pressed, and Sadie had to suppress a shudder as she looked into his eyes.

"Indeed," he snapped, spitting out his words, "this is a most sacred time of year, the birth of our Lord, and they defile it with their demonic ways. Flaunting their heathen celebrations in the faces of good Christian folk."

"Flaunting? Surely most of the celebrations happen on Inuit land. I heard you were a part of convincing the local council here not to overtly celebrate any alternative holidays."

He nodded, looking almost proud.

"Indeed, and my congregation agreed with me, as any good Christian should. Yet some of the people of Anchorage are deceived. The high school puts on a Quviasukvik day every year."

"Perhaps because some of the pupils are of Inuit heritage?" Sadie suggested. The preacher shook his head sadly at her.

"Do you really not understand, Agent," he said with a long-suffering sigh, "That there are *immortal souls* at stake here? This is not merely a question of different cultures...these are pagan customs. I would be failing in my duty as God's servant if I allowed this to continue."

Sadie allowed his words to linger in the air before she replied. "Just how far does your duty to the Lord go, Reverend Sutcliffe?" she asked in a low voice, her eyes not leaving his. Again, she saw the anger flare up in them.

Even if he wasn't their guy, this man was seriously disturbed. The thought of him having any sway over the opinions and beliefs of his congregation chilled her.

"I am not a murderer," he said in a flat voice. "I do not deny that the heathens deserve to perish...that is, if they refuse to repent. Many Inuit people renounce their pagan ways and turn to their Savior, and they are as welcome as anyone else. But those girls...they were sinners through and through."

"Because they were also prostitutes?" Sadie said bluntly. The preacher merely inclined his head, agreeing with her summation.

"They tempted many others to sin," he said, "And so yes, they earned their eternal punishment. But I was not the one who sent them to Hell, Agent. Only God decides when a life is to be taken."

"I don't think it was God who put them under the ice, Reverend," Sadie said, trying to keep a lid on her own anger. His complete lack of empathy for Verity and Eva was getting to her. Whatever happened to 'love thy neighbor?'

He didn't answer her, but the look on his face made it plain that he thought Sadie knew nothing and, as a result, was under no obligation to continue giving her his time.

"I have Evening Service to prepare for Agent, if you wouldn't mind..."

"Just a few more questions," Sadie said brusquely. Questioning him about his own beliefs was getting her nowhere, but he had also made it clear that it may not just be him who held them so strongly. "What about your 'flock?' I assume some of the congregation share your views about the 'heathens?' If you preach some of the things that you have been saying to me, I wouldn't be surprised if someone decided to take matters into their own hands."

If Sadie had thought the preacher looked angry before, it was nothing compared to the cold fury that now etched his features into a frozen grimace.

"You go too far, Agent," he hissed.

Sadie shrugged nonchalantly, even though he made every hair on her body stand on end. She had met plenty of people who had said and done terrible things, but none of them had made her want to run as much as this man, who truly believed in the righteousness of his hatred. How many others were out there who thought like him? How many whose hatred burned so brightly that they would kill for it?

"Inciting murder is a pretty big deal, Reverend," she said instead. "If you can think of anyone in your church who feels as you do but may be more inclined to act on it, then the best thing that you can do is tell us about them."

"Confidentiality between a person and their spiritual advisor is a serious matter, Agent."

"So is murder," she reminded him.

He glared at her for a long moment, and Sadie tried to read him, but it was hard to see beyond the sheer righteous indignation that poured from every fiber of him. She wasn't convinced that he was the killer; but she was also far from convinced that he wasn't.

"Whatever you may think of me and my flock, Agent," he said finally, "we are law-abiding folk. I know of no one who would commit these deeds, and I can assure you that I am not preaching murder. Thou shalt not kill. Do I preach that those sinners who do not repent will burn? Yes, I do, because that is what the Word says. Will you arrest me for that?"

Sadie felt sure that if she did, then he would thoroughly enjoy playing the persecuted martyr.

"No," she said curtly, "But if you do think of anything...I would advise you to let me, or Sheriff Cooper know. Regardless of what you say happens in the next life, Reverend, there is still a killer running around in this one. I'll let you get back to your prayers."

She turned and walked away down the middle of the pews, feeling his eyes boring into her back. As she reached the door, he called her back.

"Agent!"

She looked over her shoulder, for a split second expecting a last-minute confession. Instead, he gave her a smug smile.

"You are in the wrong place if you are looking for information on those girls. You would be better off asking at the only place where they worshipped."

Sadie frowned. "Among the Inuit, you mean?" She was already intending to ask Sheriff Cooper to accompany her to question anyone who might have known them particularly Eva, after the information that Matthew had given her. The Inuit land might be out of Cooper's jurisdiction, but she was a federal agent. And someone had to be missing these girls.

"No," the preacher responded. "Their real church. The saloon."

*

As Sadie walked into the saloon, she felt the warmer air inside hit her with relief. The temperature outside had dropped even further, and she had fought against the wind and snow just to walk from the snowcat into the bar.

The TV above the bar was on, and the news broadcast was showing an extreme weather warning. Given that the Alaskan weather tended towards the extreme at the best of times, Sadie figured there was one hell of a blizzard coming.

In spite of the weather however, there were a few familiar faces in the bar from the day before, although she was relieved to see no sign of Ted and his cronies. As she approached the counter, Caz stood up from behind it, eyeing Sadie with an equal mixture of curiosity and wariness.

"Back so soon Agent?" she said as Sadie slid onto a bar stool.

"I just wanted to ask a few questions, if you have a moment?" Sadie asked, wondering if she should have spoken to Cooper before taking it upon herself to question Caz. She suspected the Sheriff might think she was stepping on his toes, and now that things seemed to be thawing between them, she had no wish to go back to the repressed hostility of yesterday. At the same time, it was obvious that there was a friendly warmth between Caz and the Sheriff, and Sadie suspected that he may be too quick to take anything the bartender said at face value.

"Of course," Caz said, although she looked less than pleased. "Let's go and sit in the corner where it's nice and quiet, shall we? Can I get you anything to drink? On the house, of course."

"I'm fine, thank you." Sadie followed her over to a small table in the corner, next to a pool table that had seen better days. It looked as though half of the balls were missing.

"So, how can I help you? I told you everything I knew yesterday," Caz said as they sat down.

"You didn't mention Eva though, did you? I'm sure you have heard that we also found her body yesterday."

Sadie watched the other woman's reaction carefully. Caz blanched, but her gaze didn't waver.

"I guessed it might be her," she said softly. "I hoped it might be unrelated, but I knew it was too much of a coincidence, deep down."

"It seems odd that you didn't mention Eva yesterday."

"Why would I?" Caz said, looking surprised. "You only asked about Verity and Matthew. I saw Eva in here even less than Verity. She used to come in a lot, but that was before she got heavy into the drugs with Peter."

"Did you know her well, back then?" Sadie asked. Caz wrinkled her nose, making the hoop through both nostrils bounce.

"Not really. I mean, you get to know your regulars, but Eva always seemed kind of aloof. Even when I used to see her around after she was smoking meth and prostituting herself, she still had this air about her as though she thought she was better than other people. I never really warmed to her, truth be told. There was a hardness to her…the few times I saw her with Verity, I got the impression that she controlled her a bit. Not bullied her, exactly, but she was the more dominant of the two, definitely."

Sadie nodded slowly, taking in the information that Caz was giving her. "Do you think that Eva was a bad influence on Verity?"

"Definitely," Caz said with a firm nod. "Between Peter and Eva, poor Verity didn't stand a chance."

"Would you include Matthew Collins in that? Did you know that Eva was staying at his place as well?"

Caz looked thoughtful. "No, I didn't hear it mentioned, and I would have remembered. But I got that impression from Eva; that she was in and out of the area. Her mother is Inuit and lives on their land; maybe that's why Eva was aloof. A lot of them keep themselves to themselves, and I guess some of the locals prefer it that way, especially some of the old boys. They can be racist old bastards, you know?"

Sadie felt a tingle go down her spine. "Anyone in particular that you can think of?" she asked, hoping for a lead only to feel disappointed when Caz shrugged.

"Nah, not really. Just a general feeling; no different to anywhere else, really."

"I heard some of the more religious folks were uncomfortable with the Inuit customs being celebrated," Sadie said. Caz rolled her eyes.

"Yeah, like that new preacher," she said. "Although he doesn't like anyone, that one. Preaches against a new set of sinners every week, or so I've heard. One week it's the Inuit, then it's the lesbians, then the folks that call themselves Christians but don't turn up to church every Sunday. Hard man to please."

"I got that impression too," Sadie said with a smile. She found herself warming to Caz too, although at the same time she knew that she couldn't rule out anyone yet as a potential lead or assume that they were telling her the truth. People stuck together in places like this when it came to both law enforcement and outsiders – and Sadie had been away long enough to have become an outsider.

"I can't see even him doing this, though," Caz said. "I mean, it's extreme, isn't it, murder? Especially the two of them. Have you spoken to Peter Montgomery? He's a nasty piece of work, that one, although I reckon that he's nothing but a coward underneath."

"We have," Sadie said shortly, not giving anything away. She was about to ask Caz another question when the other woman sat up sharply.

"I've just remembered something," she said. "It's been niggling at me all morning; I knew there was something. It just doesn't seem right."

"What doesn't?" Sadie leaned in over the table as the woman lowered her voice.

"Like I said," Caz went on, "Eva didn't come in much anymore. The last time I saw her in here was weeks ago, and I didn't take much notice. She was with one of the locals, a fisherman… at the time I assumed he was a punter, or she had just enticed him in to buying her a few drinks…but I made a note of it, because this one is a married man, and I don't like that kind of carry on. But then it slipped my mind, until now, well, in light of who he is…"

"Who is he, Caz?" Sadie tried not to show her impatience at the other woman's excited rambling.

"Tom Willoughby," Caz said in a dramatic whisper. Sadie felt her eyes go wide.

"The guy who found Verity's body?"

Caz nodded, looking triumphant at imparting such a startling piece of information. "The very same. Like I said, I didn't think anything of it at the time but now…well, it's a bit weird, isn't it?"

“Yes, it is,” Sadie said, trying to hide her own reaction. She was eager to go and get hold of Cooper and question the man, because this opened up a whole new area of inquiry. “You’re absolutely sure that it was him? You couldn’t be mistaken?”

Caz shook her head firmly. “Completely sure. I remember now at the time, I was thinking that although it was bad behavior, I wasn’t all that surprised, because I recalled someone telling me years ago that he was partial to Inuit girls. He was with one years ago, I heard, before he met his wife. Perhaps he never got over it.”

Sadie felt her heart thudding in her chest, and she could have almost hugged the other woman. She said her goodbyes and hurried out of the saloon, barely noticing the hailstones that now pelted her from all directions. As she got into the snowcat, she radioed Cooper to fill him in, gazing out of the window and wincing as a particularly large chunk of ice hit the wind screen.

She hoped Cooper wouldn’t call off their inquiries for the day because of the weather, although she was sure that he would be as eager to follow up on this as she was. The sooner that they questioned Tom Willoughby, the better.

As far as Sadie was concerned, that meant right away.

CHAPTER SEVENTEEN

"It's just too much of a coincidence," she continued. "That he was potentially having an affair – or was a john – with Eva, and then he just happened to find Verity's body? He knows something at least. Either that, or there is something important here that we don't know."

"There's too much about this whole case that we don't know," Cooper said grimly. "I was hoping something more would come from your talk with Matthew, but maybe he and Peter really are just a dead end."

"I still think the fact that it is Quviasukvik is important.," Sadie insisted. "I wanted to talk to you about visiting the Inuit village."

"No need, I've already got it cleared," Cooper said, surprising her. Not sure whether she was pleased, or miffed that he had beaten her to it, Sadie was caught off guard when Cooper turned to her as they pulled up and gave her a slight smile.

"I'm not sure getting the preacher riled up during the holiday season was a great move, but I'm starting to think you're right; the Inuit connection could be the key. Although, we've yet to figure out what that has to do with Willoughby.

Sheriff Cooper switched off the engine.

"Nice place," Sadie said as she opened the door. Tom Willoughby lived in a large bungalow with his family on the edge of Nancy Lakes. A purple saloon car was parked outside.

"Is that his?" she asked. The Sheriff disappointed her by shaking his head.

"No. Willoughby drives a silver jeep. Nice vehicle." As they approached the door, Sadie saw the Christmas lights in the window and thought how wholesome it all looked. Unfortunately, she knew all too well that appearances could be deceptive.

Cooper knocked loudly at the door, and Sadie heard what sounded like children's voices inside.

The woman that answered the door of the large cabin looked annoyed. There was a string of Christmas decorations in her hand, and a small child tugged at her slacks.

"Mrs. Willoughby?"

"Yes, can I help you Sheriff? The Deputy already asked Tom a load of questions yesterday."

"I'm afraid we have a few more Ma'am," the Sheriff responded politely. "Could we come in?"

"Tom isn't here," she said, a stubborn set to her mouth which made the fine lines around her lips look more prominent. "He went to see his mother in Anchorage town, and he isn't back yet. Hardly surprising in this weather. I told him the tires on his truck wouldn't last another winter, but he hates spending money if he thinks he doesn't have to."

"Perhaps we could ask you a few questions?" Sadie suggested, smiling at the little girl who was watching her with her mouth open. The girl stuck her thumb between her lips and grinned back.

"We are putting up the tree," she said around her thumb. "Aren't we, Nana?"

"Yes, we are, darling," Mrs. Willoughby said in a soothing voice. "Go and give these lights to Mommy to put up while I talk to the Sheriff and the lady."

The child ran off and Mrs. Willoughby's tone reverted to its initial annoyance. "You are?" she asked Sadie. Sadie flashed her badge.

"Special Agent Price, Anchorage FBI," she said quietly, watching the woman's eyes grow wide and then flick to Cooper.

"Sheriff," she protested, "is this all necessary? Tom was so upset about finding that poor girl, I dare say it's going to ruin our Christmas as it is."

"Another body was found," Sadie said before Cooper could respond. Mrs. Willoughby looked at her, clearly outraged.

"Not by my Tom, it wasn't," she snapped. "What does it have to do with us?"

"Did you know Eva Aariak, Mrs. Willoughby?" Cooper asked, and Sadie saw the unmistakable flash of recognition in the woman's eyes before her expression shut down into a carefully blank mask which Sadie knew could mean only one thing. Anything the woman said to them now was likely to be a lie.

"No. Is that all?"

"She was the second victim. Your husband was seen drinking with her in Caz's Saloon a few weeks ago. Do you know why that would be?"

Mrs. Willoughby said nothing, but she seemed to go very, very still, as though holding her breath. Sadie saw Cooper flash her a warning look, as though advising her not to go in too hard on the woman, but Sadie already sensed this was not the time to push. There was no doubt however that their questions had hit a nerve.

"It was probably mistaken identity," Mrs. Willoughby retorted, confirming Sadie's thoughts. They would get nothing from her today. She wanted to question her further, but the woman was already shutting the door in their faces. "I will tell him to call you, Sheriff," she said, ignoring Sadie. "Now if you don't mind, I need to get back to my family."

They were left staring at the firmly closed front door. As they walked back to the snowcat, Cooper raised an eyebrow at her.

"She knows something. She recognized Eva's name. Do you think she knew about the affair?"

"If it was one." Sadie climbed into the passenger seat and shook the snow from her scarf. "Her reaction didn't strike me as that of a betrayed wife."

"Maybe she's the type to turn a blind eye and defend her guy at all costs. People stick together around here," Cooper mused.

"Not always," Sadie said, a touch of sadness tinging her voice. She ignored the look Cooper gave her, staring out of the window as he started the engine.

"Can you get the mother's address?" she asked him.

"Yes," he said, "but we will struggle to get there – or at least, get back – in this weather."

"The Inuit village then. It's not too far from here, is it? We need to speak to Eva's mother if we can. She might not even know her daughter is dead," Sadie said sadly, feeling a pang of empathy for the unknown woman.

"We do, but I'm really worried about this weather," Cooper hesitated, drumming his hands on the steering wheel as he contemplated Sadie's suggestion.

"We should try," Sadie said stubbornly as they drove back out onto the road.

Cooper sighed, but he carried on in the direction of the Inuit village rather than retracing their route. Sadie allowed herself a small smile, and tried not to look smug. If there was a missing piece to this mystery, then her instincts told her that they would find it there, not back in Anchorage.

The worsening weather, however, gave her a moment's pause. The sky was darkening fast, turning to a deep gray that looked more like twilight than late afternoon. The heavy sky felt ominous, as though hinting at more tragedy to come along with the foretold storm.

Right on cue, Golightly called her. Sadie answered, although she struggled to hear him through the howling of the wind and with an intermittent signal.

"…get back," she heard. "Have you…weather warning?"

"We're chasing up a fresh lead," Sadie said. "I'll get a report over to you as soon as I can." She heard Golightly protesting, but the line was too crackly for her to make out exactly what he was saying. Then her signal failed completely. Sadie tucked her phone back into the inner lining of her jacket, relieved at not having been ordered back. Not that she could hear clearly, anyway.

"Do you think we will make it?" she asked as the howling of the wind grew louder and was audible inside the snowcat. Cooper shrugged and changed gear, preparing to battle through the snow.

"I guess we'll find out," he said.

CHAPTER EIGHTEEN

Even with her pace slowed and head bowed by the coming storm, the girl's hips swayed as she walked. As young as she was, he noted that she already moved like one who knew how to seduce.

They all knew, of course, without needing to be told.

It was innate in them.

He licked his lips as he followed her, glancing around him. There were no other vehicles in sight other than those parked, giving him the perfect opportunity to just take her.

It was almost as though it was meant to be.

It hadn't been his intention, not yet, not so soon after the other girls, but here she was being placed right in his path.

She picked up her pace and he knew that if he was going to act then it needed to be now, before she reached her home, or before somebody appeared. Right now, the street looked deserted, giving him a window of opportunity that he might not get again for days.

He pulled alongside her and wound down his window, feeling invigorated as the cold air hit his face like a slap.

"Excuse me miss?" he called above the storm. He saw her pause and look around, smiling politely when she saw him. Her expression was trusting and friendly. Not like those other whores. They had always looked at him with contempt. Even when they were pretending to like him, pretending that they wanted him when all they wanted was money. Money to keep them in drugs and the sinful lifestyle they had become accustomed to. They thought that he was stupid, but he was cleverer than they knew.

They found that out in the end, when they were begging him for their lives.

This one, though, he could preserve her. Keep her just as she was, before the evil that was in her – that was in all of the whores – came to the fore.

She took a step towards him.

“Can I help you?” she asked. She had a dimple at the corner of her full mouth that was all shiny with lip gloss. He didn’t like that. She was too young for all that.

He would have to wipe it off.

“Can you give me directions to the hospital?” he asked. She nodded and stepped forward and he felt his heart beat faster and his groin stirring. Not that he would touch her, not in that way.

He didn’t want their filth on him.

She spoke, but he screwed his face up and cupped his hand to his ear as though he couldn’t hear her above the wind, even though he could her perfectly well.

The girl stepped even closer, and he opened the door. That should be her cue to run, if she had any sense, but she kept coming, still with that trusting smile on her face.

Hadn’t her father taught her not to go near strange men? But they were all whores underneath. It was their destiny. Her destiny.

But he was going to save her from it.

By the time she felt his grip on her arm and saw the iron bar coming towards her, it was too late.

He bundled her now unconscious frame onto the seat next to him and threw a thick blanket on top of her before driving away, looking around him before he did so.

No one had seen a thing. Abducting her had taken less than a minute.

He drove on, humming softly to himself under his breath, as he amused himself with the thought of her death.

CHAPTER NINETEEN

Sadie looked around as they approached a green painted cabin, right in the center of the Inuit village that was nestled among the bottom of the mountain range past the gorge. Although at first glance it was picturesque, set among a wild landscape otherwise populated mainly by solitary trappers and the odd grizzly, up close the cabins were rickety, with peeling paint and boarded up windows. The Inuit paid a price for their autonomy here; the village was all but poverty-stricken. It wasn't surprising, Sadie reflected, that most of the local Inuit, like her school friend Mona's family, preferred to live in the urban center of Anchorage rather than out here.

"This is where the local Inuit officer lives," Cooper told her. "He's part-time; he doubles up as a fisherman."

"Do you think he knows about the bodies yet?" Sadie asked. Cooper shrugged.

"With this weather, news broadcasts here might not be getting through. But he may have more information on the Aariaks at least. If we can manage to speak to her mother, that could fill in some gaps."

Sadie nodded as she followed Cooper to the door of the cabin, bracing herself against the inevitable shock of the subzero temperatures outside. Up here, coming down from the mountains and whirling through the pine trees, the wind sounded even louder and more fierce. There was a mournful quality to its howling that sent a shiver up Sadie's spine.

"I hope he's in," Cooper muttered under his breath as they waited at the door.

"I seriously doubt that anyone else is silly enough to be out in this," Sadie replied, hoping they weren't going to end up stranded out here and without having achieved anything.

They were about to give up and go back to the snowcat when the door creaked open. A guy in his forties frowned at them, then frowned even deeper when he saw the Sheriff.

"Sheriff Cooper, isn't it? What brings you here...out of your jurisdiction, aren't you?"

"Officer Kolit, good to see you. I cleared it with your elders a few hours ago," Cooper replied. "Two Inuit girls have gone missing – one of them you may be familiar with."

Kolit's eyes flew up his forehead. "No-one told me anything about anything," he grumbled.

Cooper gave him a quick rundown of the case, and the girls names. As they had hoped, they saw the recognition on his face when they mentioned Eva's last name.

"I know the Aariaks. Nice family. Most of them moved away years ago after old John Aariak died, but his youngest, Yura, is still here. She's Eva's mother."

Cooper and Sadie exchanged glances. "Does she keep in touch with Eva, do you know?" Sadie asked. Kolit nodded.

"I believe so, although she doesn't come back here too often. I guess you guys already know about Eva's lifestyle? The drugs?"

"We do, yes," Sadie said. "It's common knowledge, then?"

"People talk, but Yura keeps herself to herself. I know because she confided in me a few years ago, told me that Eva was on meth and had shacked up with some pimp near Anchorage. She was devastated, as you can imagine. She wanted me to help, but what can anyone really do? Eva was an adult by then. I tried to speak to her when I saw her, but I think it did more harm than good," he admitted sadly. "She didn't come back here for a while after that."

"Can you take us to Yura?" Cooper asked.

"Sure; she lives in the next cabin," Kolit said.

Sadie started to follow Kolit, her stomach sinking. She wasn't looking forward to telling Yura Aariak that her daughter wouldn't be coming home for the holidays after all.

*

"She was such a good girl," Yura sobbed, gripping Sadie's hand tightly. "Always so polite, and so helpful. Until she moved to the city, and she met that guy...he promised her the world. I told her, don't make the mistake I did, but she wouldn't listen..." the woman's voice became incoherent, her sobbing taking over from her words, and Sadie wished she hadn't been the one to break the news to the poor woman. She felt desperately sad for her, and underneath that, angry. Angry at whoever had such blatant disregard for human life that they had taken this woman's only child. And not just her but Verity, too.

And maybe others. With Peter and Matty not showing any more promise as suspects, Sadie was growing more and more convinced that, whoever had killed the girls, it was about more than a drug deal gone wrong or a crime of passion. She remembered the hatred that she had seen in the eyes of the preacher and knew he would not be the only one.

"Did you question him?" Yura said suddenly, her head snapping up and her eyes blazing with fury. "Peter, his name was."

"Yes," Sadie said, carefully extracting her hand from Yura's. The older woman had dug her nails so deep into Sadie's palm that she was surprised they hadn't drawn blood. "Do you think he may have had something to do with it?"

"I never met him," Yura said, "But he got her on drugs, and convinced her to sell herself. Who else could it be? The last time I saw her she said that she had left him, and she was going to turn her life around. She had a friend she was going to bring back for the festival. She was part Inuit too, she said."

"Verity Hagen?" Sadie asked. Yura nodded.

"Verity's body was also found, in one of the Lynx Lakes," Cooper cut in, and Yura howled in disbelief before bursting into tears again. Cooper looked uncomfortable, and relieved when Kolit, who had been standing quietly at the back of the room, stepped forward.

"If there is anything you can tell them, Yura, anything that you think might be important..." He looked at Sadie. "It's not often that outside officers take such an interest in our girls, to be honest. Especially not ones in...Eva's position," he said delicately. "I certainly wouldn't expect to see FBI on the case."

"We're going to do everything we can to find whoever did this," Sadie said, her voice ringing with determination. "Did Eva say anything to indicate Peter might hurt her?" she asked Yura, who was still crying, but more quietly now, the tears flowing down her cheeks.

"No, not really," Yura admitted. "But who else could want to hurt her? She was such a sweet girl. Everyone loved her."

Sadie remembered Caz's assessment of Eva and wondered if Yura had really known the woman that her daughter had become, or if Caz had just taken against the girl.

Eva was seen a few weeks ago with a man named Tom Willoughby," Sadie went on. "Did she ever mention him?"

She was surprised when Yura sat up straight, a sudden smile breaking through her tears. "Tom?" she said. "So he did keep his promise to meet her. I was sure that wife of his would put a stop to it, just like she always did when Eva was a little girl. Didn't want him anywhere near me, did she, even though we were over well before he met her. She never liked the fact that he had an Inuit girl, wouldn't let Eva meet her precious kids," she said bitterly.

"You're saying that Tom Willoughby was Eva's *father*?" the Sheriff cut in. Yura nodded.

"Yes. She never saw him growing up, because he had his new family, but then he tracked her down when she was eighteen, but of course she didn't want to know him then. But she made contact a few months ago, she found out his favorite fishing spot and went to see him a few times, and he promised her he would meet up with her regularly, even introduce her to her siblings. I didn't believe him, if I'm honest."

So, Eva had met Tom up at his fishing spot. That would explain the ribbon, if it was hers, Sadie thought. She shook her head to clear it, trying to make sense of this sudden twist in their investigation.

"Did she say if they had argued at all recently?" she asked gently. "Or if he was scared of his wife finding out?"

Yura put a hand to her mouth, looking shocked. "You can't think it was Tom, surely?" she said.

"We have to pursue every avenue, Ms. Aariak."

Yura shook her head. "It wasn't Tom," she said firmly. "He would never have hurt Eva, not in a million years. He was always a gentle, gentle man. Oh, too much of a coward where that wife of his is concerned, I don't doubt that, but I'm telling you he wouldn't harm a soul, least of all his own daughter."

"People change over the years," Sadie said, but Yura shook her head stubbornly. "Not Tom," she insisted.

"Have you seen Tom today?" she asked, thinking of the tracks in the snow.

"No," Yura looked puzzled.

"Did Tom know Verity?" Cooper asked, changing tack.

"I have no idea," Yura asked, shaking her head. For a moment, she looked angry. "Why are you asking me all these questions about Tom?" she demanded. "You should be out there, catching whoever did this to my beautiful girl and her friend!"

"That's what the Sheriff and Agent Price are trying to do, Yura," Kolit said softly. Yura looked suspiciously at Sadie.

"Why?" she asked abruptly. "Why do you care so much that you're up here in this weather? Since when do the feds care about girls like my Eva? What aren't you telling me?"

"We're telling you all we know," Sadie said, feeling a wave of compassion for the woman. She could understand her anger and knew from experience that it was an emotion that was so much easier to feel than grief. That would come later, when Yura was alone, when it would break over her like a tidal wave.

And it would never truly leave her.

Steeling her mind against her own memories, suddenly all too fresh in the face of Yura's pain, Sadie resumed her questions.

"I know this is hard," she said, "and I want you to know that we do care, and we are going to do everything we can. That's why anything that you can think of that Eva might have mentioned could be vital information. Anyone that she had an argument with, or that Verity had, or anything she was worried about...it's all important, no matter how trivial."

Yura's anger eased, and she tipped her head to one side like a bird, her eyes far away as she thought over Sadie's words. Finally, she shook her head, looking crushed.

"She didn't tell me much about her life, really. I always told her I didn't want to know about the drugs and... the other stuff. The last time I saw her, just over a week ago, she was happy. She was in contact with her father, had stayed away from that Peter and was coming to stay for Quviasukvik," Yura's face crumpled with a fresh sob. "She told me she was getting clean."

"Do you think that was true?" Sadie asked, trying to sound diplomatic even as she thought about the fresh meth burns on Eva's body. Yura gave a bitter little laugh.

"No. I could tell that she was still using just as bad. But I didn't challenge her on it. I was just glad to see her and that she seemed happier. If I had known what was going to happen...I could have done something." She broke down again, despair cracking her voice in two.

"It wasn't your fault, there was nothing that you could have done," Sadie whispered, knowing that there was nothing she could say that would ease the woman's pain one iota. That she would always blame herself, even if there was no logical reason to do so. Just as, for years, Sade had tormented herself with thoughts of her last days with Jessica, wondering if there was something that she could have done or said differently that could have somehow changed her sister's fate.

It was the not knowing what had truly happened that was the hardest thing to bear.

"Just a few more questions, Ms. Aariak," Cooper said, and for once Sadie was happy for him to take over. The tiny cabin seemed suddenly claustrophobic, and Sadie was struggling to keep her own feelings in check. Yura nodded, wiping her eyes.

"I know it's a difficult subject," Cooper said, clearing his throat, "but if there's anything you know about Eva's customers, or anything she said, that would be really helpful. Anyone who creeped her out maybe, or any regulars she might have mentioned."

Yura shook her head. "I told you," she said miserably, "I didn't ask her about all that. What mother would want to know?"

"I understand," Cooper said. "But if you think of anything..."

Yura looked over at the Inuit officer. "You should try that cousin of yours," she said bitterly. "He's always been one for the hookers. I've caught him sniffing around my Eva before."

Sadie looked over at Kolit, who looked embarrassed at Yura's outburst. "My cousin, Eddie," he explained. "He's a trapper. Too much time on his own; he's developed a drink problem. Yura's right, there are always rumors about him going to Anchorage to pick up girls."

"Our Inuit girls too, I've heard," Yura said in disgust. "Eva never mentioned him," she added to Sadie, "but it wouldn't surprise me if he knew something. Sorry, John," she said to Kolit, "but he's a nasty piece of work."

John Kolit didn't look as though he was about to argue. "Could you take us to see Eddie?" Cooper asked. The officer nodded.

"Sure. He's got a shack just at the edge of the village. He had another one down at the gorge, but he doesn't use it anymore."

Cooper shot Sadie a look, and she nodded at him as they had the same realization.

They had found their missing trapper.

CHAPTER TWENTY

Sadie peered around the dusty shack, trying to see through the gloom. Like the abandoned place up at the gorge, dried pelts hung from the ceiling, casting shadows across the small building. Among them stood Eddie Kolit, his arms folded obstinately in front of his chest as his cousin spoke to him in urgent, hushed tones.

They were speaking in Inuit and the Sheriff was listening with a suspicious look on his face. Sadie, however, had a rough knowledge of the basics, largely thanks to her childhood friendship with Mona, and was satisfied that their conversation consisted of no more than the officer trying to convince his cousin to answer their questions. Eddie had no intention of playing ball; in fact, he was downright hostile, insisting that Sadie and Cooper had no right to question him on Inuit land.

The conversation seemed to be going round in circles. Sadie stepped forward, flashing her badge. "Special Agent Price," she said politely. "I'm with the FBI, so yes, in a case like this I do have jurisdiction, Eddie."

Realizing that Sadie had been able to understand him, Eddie flushed crimson and glared at Sadie, still not saying a word to either her or Cooper. Instead, he turned back to his cousin.

"I don't know anything about any missing girls," he said, still in Inuit. "Least of all Yura's daughter. She should have kept a better eye on her and maybe she wouldn't have gone wild."

"So you did know Eva?" Sadie responded, this time using Inuit herself. She saw Cooper look at her curiously.

Eddie shrugged. "Not well. I saw her about, growing up. You could tell that she was going to be…trouble." He said the last word with a knowing leer that made Sadie bristle, and even his cousin looked at him in disgust.

"So you weren't ever a customer of hers?"

Eddie glowered at her. "What are you trying to say?" Anger made him speak more quickly, and Sadie had to listen carefully to make out the words. Her language skills were rusty; it had been a long time since she had spoken or heard the Native Alaskan language.

"We were told that you're a frequent customer of sex workers in and around Anchorage," Sadie said, this time in English for Cooper's benefit, as the Sheriff looked confused as he tried to follow what was happening.

"You were told wrong," Eddie snapped, still speaking in Inuit. "Maybe when I was younger, but not now. And I wouldn't have gone near the Aariak girl, not with her drug use. They get diseases, the junkies. Everyone knows that."

"When was the last time you saw Eva?" Kolit cut in.

Eddie shrugged. "Dunno. Months ago, in the village when she was visiting Yura. She looked wasted." He said the last with contempt, which Sadie thought was hypocritical given the strong smell of whiskey coming off the man.

"Did you know Verity Hagen?" she asked. Eddie looked blank.

"Who?"

"She was a friend of Eva's. They lived together…and worked together. She was part Inuit too."

"Never heard of her," Eddie snapped. He looked at Kolit again, anger blazing in his bloodshot eyes. "Why are you bringing these people here, John? Letting them tramp around our land uninvited, asking their nosy questions. Our girls are our business."

"Eva and Verity have been murdered," Sadie said tightly before Kolit could answer, "That makes it our business. And it's our job to catch the person responsible."

"Why don't you go and do that, then?" Eddie sneered at her. "Instead of coming here and harassing me. Looking for one of us to pin it all on, are you, rather than admit it will be a white guy? Ain't it always? Our girls go missing all the time and none of you give a shit."

"I give a shit," Sadie retorted, "and I will be questioning anyone who I believe might know something, regardless of who they are. Right now, you're just being obstructive. Have you got something to hide, Eddie?"

Eddie's eyes nearly popped out of his face, and he looked angry enough to explode. Kolit raised a hand and told him to calm down as Sheriff Cooper stepped closer to Sadie. She found that she was grateful for his presence.

"Would you like to fill me in on what's being said here?" he said calmly, his eyes fixed on Eddie.

"He says he has never heard of Verity and doesn't really know Eva. The last time he saw her was months ago in the village," Sadie repeated.

"Mr. Kolit," Cooper said politely. "Could you tell us why you are not using your shack at the gorge anymore?"

Eddie just glared at him.

"Eddie, just answer the Sheriff," Kolit said wearily. "There's nothing wrong with your English." The officer looked apologetically at them, and Sadie guessed that this wasn't the first time he had found himself apologizing for his wayward cousin.

"What does that have to do with you?" Eddie answered after a pause.

"Eva Aariak's body was found in the lake right outside your hut, Mr. Kolit," Cooper told him. Eddie looked shocked, and Sadie studied his face, wondering if he looked almost too shocked. The shock of someone who wasn't expecting the body he had drowned miles away to wash up on his doorstep, perhaps?

"Well, that's a shame," he said eventually, giving himself a little shake as though to collect his thoughts. "But I still don't see what it's got to do with me? I haven't used the shack there for weeks. It's more suitable for the summer. Conditions at this time of year are bad around the gorge. I wouldn't want to be caught up there in a storm like this, would I?" he added as the wind suddenly howled outside, causing the small windows in the shack to rattle furiously in their wooden frames.

"Do you spend much time around Nancy Lakes?" the Sheriff asked. Eddie sneered again.

"What, with the tourists? No, Officer, I don't. You're wasting your time coming here to question me. I might be a lot of things, but a murderer I ain't. You want to be looking at your own community." The look of disgust on his face was palpable.

"What makes you say that, Eddie?" Sadie asked. "Are you thinking of anyone in particular? Or any group, maybe?"

Eddie looked puzzled for a moment and then shrugged. "No, I keep myself to myself and my own people. I don't know who did this. But what I do know is, it will be one of your lot that has killed those girls. It's always been your lot killing us, whether it's for land or religion or kicks. Whoever this guy is, he's just finishing up the genocide you lot started." He spat his words out, and the hatred on his face was so potent that Sadie had to stop herself taking a step back, away from the force of it. Although his grudge may have more justification behind it, there was something in the way he spoke that reminded her of the preacher from this morning.

It was the kind of hatred that prompted people to kill.

"Eddie," Kolit said, his voice low but angry, "Sheriff Cooper and Agent Price are here at my request and with my permission. They're doing their best to catch this maniac. They haven't hurt anyone."

Eddie snorted and spat on the ground in front of them.

"Get out," he snapped. "I'm done talking to either of you."

"I just have a few more questions, Mr. Kolit," Cooper said smoothly, seemingly unfazed by the man's vitriol.

"Yeah? Well, I'm not answering them. I want you off my property, and unless Miss FBI here has some kind of warrant, then you have to leave, don't you?"

Eddie turned around and stomped to the back of the shack, where he picked up a pelt he was working on. He started humming to himself, clearly telling them that their conversation was over. Officer Kolit looked at Sadie apologetically.

"I'm sorry about Eddie," he said quietly. "He can be difficult, and he doesn't like outsiders. If he tells me anything useful, rest assured I'll let you know. I'll be asking around too. Some of Eva's old friends here might know something."

"Thank you," Sadie said and followed him and Cooper outside.

She didn't bother saying goodbye to Eddie, but as they left, she heard him call out to them in Inuit, almost mockingly, "Beware the *Muhaha*. He will kill you too."

Sadie didn't reply.

They had to fight through the wind and the driving wall of snow to get back to their vehicles, and any attempt to say goodbye to Kolit was lost in the screeching howl of the blizzard. As Sadie clambered into her seat the wind nearly pulled her back out of the cab, but Cooper leaned forward and grabbed her arm, hauling her in.

"Thanks," Sadie mumbled as she righted herself on the seat. "This is some crazy blizzard. Are you going to be all right to drive back?"

The track ahead was barely visible, and it was only going to get worse.

"I'll have to be," Cooper said, sounding worried himself. Then he changed the subject. "What was it that Eddie shouted to us as we were leaving?" he asked. "I caught the word for 'beware.' Beware what?"

"The *Muhaha*," Sadie replied. "It's an old Inuit legend about a monster or demon that comes out at night, in the height of winter. Tall and thin and looks to be made of ice himself. He's a killer."

"I think I've heard something about that round town," Cooper said thoughtfully. "The kids call it the 'iceman'?"

Sadie nodded and shuddered to herself as Cooper pulled off, replaying Eddie's words in her head.

Beware the iceman. He will kill you too.

CHAPTER TWENTY ONE

We're not going to make it.

For the first time since she had been assigned to this case, Sadie was starting to feel scared by the extreme weather conditions. Up until now it had been merely a backdrop, an inconvenience that she had expected, having grown up and lived through harsher storms than this. Her main concern had been that it might push them off the case in the crucial first few days. But now, as Cooper drove as fast as he possibly could against the storm that was trying to beat them back, Sadie wondered if they could really be in danger. The storm was getting worse, and they would soon be outrun and unable to battle any further through it.

"We'll get there," Cooper said, making Sadie jump. He seemed to have read her mind.

"I hope so," Sadie said, staring out of the window. All she could see was snow against an increasingly inky sky.

"What, are you doubting my driving?" Cooper joked, although she could hear his own anxiety lacing through the humor. Sadie tried to laugh, then tried not to scream as something hit the front of the car.

"Just a falling branch," Cooper said. Sadie glanced at his hands on the wheel. He was gripping it so hard that his usually tanned knuckles were white.

"So, what did you think? Back at the village?" she asked him, more to take their minds off the storm outside than anything else.

Cooper looked thoughtful.

"The trapper seems like an angry guy, but so far there's no motive other than Yura suggesting he was a punter, which may or may not be true. That comment at the end though – do you think he was threatening you?"

"Probably just trying to scare me," Sadie said, not wanting to admit that his words had indeed deeply unnerved her. "Still, he's worth watching. Maybe Kolit can find out something more useful. But I'm more interested in the fact that Tom Willoughby was Eva's father. As soon as we can, we need to speak to him. If it was his tracks in the snow, then he obviously doesn't want to speak to us. I would say he's our biggest lead right now."

"What did you think of the wife? Do you think she could have done it?" Cooper asked. "We've been looking for a man, but maybe that's a mistake?"

"Maybe," Sadie mused. "Yura said that she was jealous of Eva. She might well have wanted to kill her to get rid of her from Tom's life, but what would be her motive for killing Verity?"

"Wrong place, wrong time?" Cooper suggested. "It seems likely they were killed together."

"Would Mrs. Willoughby have been strong enough to subdue them both and hold them under the water though?" Sadie said doubtfully. "Both girls were frail, but Mrs. Willoughby didn't look particularly strong. Although," she added from experience, "that can be deceptive. Especially when someone is motivated by rage." She gave a heavy sigh. "We have more questions than answers so far."

Cooper took his eyes off the road for a moment to glance at Sadie.

"We'll find him, Price," he said, determination in his voice. "Or her, as the case may be."

Sadie couldn't help a wry smile. "We?" she teased. "We've come a long way from yesterday."

Cooper shrugged. "You're not so bad," he grinned. "I guess I can put up with you for a little while."

"I'm not so sure your sister feels the same way."

Cooper looked uncomfortable. "Jane can be…protective of me. And very territorial. But the things she said to you yesterday, about your sister, they were wrong. I spoke to her about it last night. She's sorry; although I doubt you will hear it from her."

Sadie was silent for a moment. Somehow, Jessica just kept coming up, and for some reason the thought of her sister brought Eddie's words back to her. *Beware of the iceman.* She thought of her dream the night before, and of the shadowy figure who had carried her sister away through the snow. It hadn't been like that in real life, of course. She hadn't known that Jessica was missing until the morning. And even then, she had assumed her sister had sneaked out to see a boy. Their father didn't let them have boyfriends, especially Jessica. He had cared less about what Sadie got up to, while simultaneously being quick to blame her for everything.

"It's okay," she said, realizing that Cooper was waiting for her to say something. "I can understand how it looks…but my past shouldn't overshadow this case. This is different."

She heard the hollow ring to her words and knew that she didn't really believe them even as she spoke them. Cooper, too, looked doubtful.

"I don't want to upset you," he said, "But do you think so? Really? I mean, assuming this isn't anything to do with the Willoughby's family drama or a drug deal gone wrong…if we're just talking about some maniac who's drowning girls…it is a hell of a coincidence, isn't it?"

Sadie pulled in her breath and let it out on a long exhale. In some ways she wanted to talk about it, and to share her burning desire to find her sister's killer, but she wasn't entirely sure that she could trust Logan Cooper, not yet.

"I guess it is," she said, her voice shaky. "The same lakes, too…we found Jessica in the Lynx loop, just down from where Verity surfaced. But that loop covers a pretty big area, and some of the smaller lakes up in the mountains could be linked too."

Cooper nodded. "Which, of course, is one of the problems in this case. We can't be certain where they were actually drowned."

Sadie frowned, thinking. "There must be a pattern to the currents, though, right? Isn't there a way of mapping that sort of thing?"

"Maybe you could ask your boss?" Cooper suggested. "That sounds like it would need someone with some pretty technical kit. We could get the information easily enough, but it's deciphering it, that's the issue."

"What about the ice fishermen? Especially the Inuit. There must be locals with that sort of knowledge, before I have to go asking Golightly for a hike in the budget. I mean, how did people cope before the days of infrared and satellites?"

Cooper nodded, acquiescing her point. She felt relieved that the conversation had steered away from the subject of Jessica.

Until his next question brought it straight back.

"Was anything like that tried with your sister?"

"No," Sadie said shortly. "There was an investigation at first…but it was dropped. It was never officially classed as a murder, there just wasn't enough evidence." She felt the familiar cold anger rising up in her the way it had on the day that she had been told that news. That no one would ever be held to account for the fact that Jessica was gone.

Her father had received the news without saying a word. Then he had walked out, no doubt to go to the saloon, leaving a fifteen-year-old Sadie on her own. She had slept with her drawers pushed up against her bedroom door that night, expecting him to come home in a rage and beat his frustration and grief into her. He hadn't, but instead had pretty much ignored her existence until she had left Alaska for college. They hadn't spoken since. She had sent Christmas cards for the first few years but had stopped when she never got a response. She wondered if she had ever really expected one.

"But you think it was?" Cooper asked, interrupting her thoughts.

"Yes. Jessica was sensible, always. She wouldn't have gone wandering around by the lakes on her own, especially in the winter, and at night."

Cooper cleared his throat, looking awkward. "Did you ever think…."

"That she might have killed herself?" Sadie finished for him, her voice sharp. "No. She never would have. The police at the time suggested it, people whispered it…but I knew my sister. That's not what happened. She was murdered. Don't ask me how I know; I just do, and I always have." She curled her hands into fists and felt the edges of her fingernails digging into her palms. "And the killer is still out there somewhere."

The atmosphere in the snowcat felt charged with tension, and for a few long moments neither of them spoke.

"What did your sister look like?" Cooper asked, and Sadie knew instantly what he was getting at.

"She didn't look Inuit. We're not; my great-grandparents were Italian and Irish," she said. "She did have the long black hair though. Jessica was darker than I am. Prettier."

Sadie turned her face to the window, blinking back sudden tears and inwardly cursing Cooper for starting this. She wasn't going to cry in front of him, she thought fiercely.

"Sadie, I'm sorry," Cooper said. "I didn't mean to upset you."

Sadie was about to reply, to tell him that it was fine, and she was fine, even though she wasn't fine at all, when there was another, louder thump on the front of the vehicle. Cooper cursed and turned the wheel, only for the snowcat to suddenly skid out of his control. Sadie stared out of the window to see a wall of white coming towards them and realized they were heading straight for a huge snowbank.

"Hold on!" Cooper shouted. Sadie braced herself for the crash.

When it came, it knocked all of the breath from her body, and her vision went black. She was vaguely aware of the hiss of the airbags being deployed.

And then, nothing.

CHAPTER TWENTY TWO

Sadie's eyelids flickered as she resurfaced from what felt like a deep yet troubled sleep. As she opened her eyes, blinking in confusion, she remembered the crash and jerked upwards in her seat, flinching as pain shot through her head. Bringing her hand to her forehead she felt a small gash, but nothing too serious. Gingerly, she stretched her legs. They seemed to be working.

"Cooper?"

Sadie turned to see the Sheriff slumped in the front seat, his eyes closed and his skin a gray pallor. There was a fierce looking gash at his right temple that looked a lot more serious than her own cut. Her breath caught in her throat as she reached for his neck to feel for a pulse. It was there, and steady. She exhaled in relief, but it was short lived when he didn't respond to her calling him.

"Okay, don't panic," she murmured to herself, forcing herself to think practically and assess the situation. The snowcat hadn't turned over, which was something to be relieved about, but had spun straight into a snow bank which she could see through the window was largely blocking the doors. Not that there would have been any point in getting out. The storm was still at its height, and they were miles from anywhere that help could be found.

It was also freezing. Thin tendrils of ice were creeping over the inside of the front window screen, and her breath hovered in front of her in small plumes. She clapped her hands together and stamped her feet to bring some warmth back into them before reaching for her radio, praying that she would be able to get a signal.

Loud crackling sounded, along with a muffled voice in the background that she could barely hear.

"This is Agent Price," she said loudly and urgently into the radio. "S.O.S. Myself and Sheriff Cooper are in a crash on the road between the Inuit village and the Lynx Loop gorge. About thirty minutes away from the lakes. Temperatures subzero. Sheriff Cooper is unconscious with a cut to the head. Please send emergency assistance. I repeat, send emergency assistance."

The line crackled back at her, this time with no audible voice, and then went dead. Sadie tried again, but the signal had gone.

She pushed against the door, using all of her strength to get it open, and causing snow to come tumbling into the vehicle into the process. She slid out, glancing back at the Sheriff.

"Just hold on, Cooper," she told him, knowing that he wouldn't hear her. "It's going to be all right. We're going to be all right."

She had to believe that. There was no way that she had come all the way back to Alaska just to be taken out by hypothermia.

But battling through the snow was next to impossible. The bank was nearly as tall as her and Sadie knew that all she was doing was making herself colder. They were in the middle of nowhere, with not a soul to be seen, just miles and miles of sparkling ice.

But she had to try. She cupped her hands around her mouth and yelled as loudly as she could.

"Help!"

Then again, and again, before she waited, straining to hear any sound back.

There was nothing apart from the faint echo of her own voice.

Sadie made her way back inside the snowcat, hauling herself into the seat and forcing the door shut. Doing so dislodged the snow on the branch that had hit the car and it slid down the window in a solid lump. Sadie sat back and sighed.

There was nothing that she could do but wait, and hope.

Replacing the radio, she leaned her head back on her seat and tucked her legs up, huddling into herself for warmth. She watched the Sheriff, alert for any change in his condition, willing him to wake up. She had a vague memory of watching a TV show about rescue services, and how a woman had stopped her friend from slipping into a deathly coma by talking to him. Sadie wasn't sure if talking to an unconscious Sheriff was going to prevent either of them from hypothermia, but if she didn't attempt to pass the time, she would go crazy.

So, she told him about Jessica.

"You wanted to know about my sister," she said, her voice sounding loud inside the car. "Honestly, where do I start? The thing is, my memories of her now are always overshadowed by how she died and the day that she was found. How it felt when I realized that I was never going to see her again. And of course, that's all anyone ever wants to know about, isn't it? Her death. Even you."

Sadie took a deep breath and looked out of the window without seeing the landscape around her. Instead, she saw into the past.

"I wish I could just remember her as she was when she was alive," she said, and smiled as she had a vivid image of Jessica laughing, her long dark hair falling over her face. "Because she was the best thing in my life, she really was. Every plan I ever made for the future; she was in it. It never occurred to me that she wouldn't be around. Why would it?"

Sadie took a deep breath and a single tear fell from her eye. It froze on her cheek.

"Jessica was *good*, you know? In a way I never was, that few people are, really. She was the kindest person I've ever met. I know everyone says this about their loved ones who have died, but there really was something special about her. I mean," Sadie laughed bitterly, "Even my father loved her, and if you knew him you would never think him capable of the emotion. Not that it stopped him spending all our money on drink or mostly leaving us to fend for ourselves, but still, she was the only person other than himself that I think he ever really cared about."

Sadie fell silent for a moment, remembering. There was so much to remember.

"She used to love this time of year. We would get the bus – when it was actually running, you know? – into Anchorage to see the lights, and then she would take me for a hot chocolate in this little café on the High Street. She had this weekend job in one of the fishing tackle shops, and she would use the money to take me out. I always had the gingerbread flavor, and she had white chocolate. Every single time. With whipped cream and marshmallows and chocolate sprinkles. And we would just sit and watch the world go by.

"She loved it in the town; she used to beg Dad to move closer to actual civilization, instead of being stuck out in the hinterlands. We had a few school friends dotted around, but it was always such a hike to meet up. And then there was never anywhere to go, except skating, but she was never keen on skating.

"That's how I know her death wasn't an accident," she said as her recollections took an inevitably darker turn. "She would never have been reckless on the lakes. She was more sensible than that. Every time I went out without her to the lakes or the groves she would always worry, even though I knew my way around better than she did. I always loved the wilderness.

“After she died,” Sadie said sadly, “I couldn’t stand the sight of it. After Quantico I took my first position in Florida. You don’t how good it was to not see snow and ice every day. To actually be *hot*. Jessica would have loved it there.”

Sadie fell silent, listening to the howling of the wind. It seemed to have died down a little, but perhaps that was just wishful thinking. As her memories retreated again, she realized how cold and numb her whole body felt. She could barely feel her feet or hands, and she felt the fear rising up in her.

They could die here.

And the killer will never be found, she thought bitterly, and she was unsure herself whether she meant the victims’ killer, or Jessica’s.

Assuming they weren’t one and the same. Sheriff Cooper voicing the very thing that she had been trying not to consciously confront in any depth had brought her suspicions sharply into focus. Hearing Cooper express it somehow validated her own hunches. The similarities were too stark to ignore.

But if they weren’t rescued, and soon, then she would never get the chance to investigate them.

She had to get out of this. They had to get out of this.

She glanced over at Cooper, feeling a rush of concern. They had just begun to work well together, and to establish the start of a rapport that had seemed impossible the day before. Her heart ached at the thought of him never waking up.

Sadie stared out of the window, weighing up how far it would be possible to get before she succumbed to the cold. The chances of coming across anyone who could help were slim to none, but she was out of options.

Just then, a horn sounded in the distance. Gasping, Sadie hit the snowcat horn and then wrenched and pushed at the door, fighting against the snow.

“Help!” she screamed, but the wind took her voice.

Then the horn came gain, louder and closer. The vehicle was heading towards them. Sadie pressed her face up against the glass and cried with relief as she saw a large snow trawler with a front plow emerging through the whiteness. As it got closer, she made out the two figures in the cab. The ice harvester, Mac, was driving, and Deputy Jane Cooper sat next to him, her face etched with worry. Sadie wiped the tears from her cheeks as she watched them pull up and get out, their faces now all but covered with scarves. They ran over to the snowcat, and the Deputy clapped a hand to her mouth as she caught sight of her brother.

"His pulse is steady, but he's unresponsive," Sadie told her as the Deputy and Mac hurriedly wrenched open Cooper's door.

"We need to get him to a hospital," Mac said. Between the three of them they eased the Sheriff from the cab, then Mac and the Deputy carried him to the trawler. Sadie clambered out of the snowcat only to nearly fall into the snow as her numb legs nearly gave way. She staggered to her feet and towards the trawler. The Deputy came back for her.

"Lean on my shoulder," Jane Cooper said. Sadie smiled at her weakly.

"I never thought I would be so grateful to see you," she joked, gladly taking the other woman up on her offer. Jane helped her into the cab before getting in after her, slamming the door shut against the cold. The inside of the cab was blissfully warm, and Sadie felt her circulation gradually coming back. She would be lucky, she thought, not to have frostbite.

Before they pulled off, Mac handed her a flask of hot, sugary cocoa and Sadie gulped at it, closing her eyes as the warm liquid hit the back of her throat.

"Thank you, guys," she said quietly. "I was worried that the message hadn't got through."

"Thank God it did," the Deputy said, looking at her brother laid out on the seat behind. They had thrown a warm fur over him, but his skin still had a blue tinge, although his breath, Sadie noted, looked stronger.

"He's going to be okay," she said with more certainty than she felt.

They rumbled back towards the hospital, Mac's eyes determinedly fixed on the road ahead. Although the storm was indeed slowing, conditions were just as treacherous. The trawler was up to the job but moving slower than Sadie would have liked given the Sheriff's condition.

Next to her, the Deputy was stiff with anxiety as she looked over at her brother every few minutes. More to distract her than anything else, Sadie asked, "Any new developments today? We've got a lot to fill you in on."

The other woman looked at her with an expression that made Sadie's heart feel as though it had sunk to her stomach.

"I was going to wait until we had gotten you checked out, but…" Jane gnawed at her bottom lip.

"What is it?" Sadie asked. The Deputy's next words confirmed her worst fears.

"Another girl has gone missing."

Sadie closed her eyes briefly and took a deep breath. The crash had shocked and scared her but processing those feelings would now have to wait. This was more important.

"Another sex worker?"

"No," Jane told her, "A schoolgirl. A senior. She never came home from school, even though her friends saw her get off the bus and walk towards her street."

Sadie frowned. "Are we sure there's a connection? She's only been missing a matter of hours. Teenagers do go AWOL. She could turn up at a boyfriend's place."

The Deputy shook her head.

"Doubtful. She's a Grade A student who has never been in trouble. It would be completely out of character, according to her friends and parents."

Sadie nodded her head slowly, still unsure. Plenty of parents said that about their children, only for their supposed golden child to turn up with a guy or be out on a drug binge somewhere. But the look on the other woman's face told Sadie that she was missing something, and she had an awful feeling that she knew exactly what that was.

"What's her name?" she asked.

"Masha Trent," Jane replied.

"And is she….?"

"Yes," Jane told her, her eyes wide. "Masha is half Inuit."

CHAPTER TWENTY THREE

Sadie stared out of the window as they approached the hospital. Her mind was whirling with emotions as she grappled with what Jane had told her. Another – potential- victim was somewhere out there in the cold.

Possibly already dead.

The fact that Masha had Inuit heritage seemed to confirm Sadie's original hunch, yet there was an important difference between this girl and the other two victims. She was no sex worker or drug addict, but an innocent-sounding schoolgirl.

Just like Jessica.

"We're here," Mac said, his gruff voice cutting through her thoughts. They had radioed ahead, and already two paramedics were coming towards the trawler with a stretcher.

Behind them came a cough.

"Logan!" the Deputy cried, spinning round. Sadie watched as the Sheriff opened his eyes and looked at them. His eyes were slightly unfocused, but he seemed aware of his surroundings and the color had returned to his face.

"Logan, can you hear me?" his sister asked. The Sheriff nodded and then winced in pain.

"Try not to move," Sadie said quickly. "We're at the hospital. You're going to be fine."

"What happened?" he asked weakly.

"A branch landed on the snowcat and we ran into a bank. You've hit your head," Sadie told him.

"It hurts," he said, and closed his eyes again.

The paramedics were at the trawler now and the Deputy jumped out and opened the back door of the trawler for them. They got the Sheriff onto the stretcher and carried him into the Emergency Room, Sadie and Jane following.

They walked into the ER and caught up with where the Sheriff was now being lifted onto a trolley to be triaged. He was talking with the nurse, although his voice was weak and shaky. As Sadie approached, he reached out and weakly squeezed her hand.

"Thank you," he said.

"I didn't do anything," Sadie shrugged. "I was in that snowcat with you."

Cooper looked right into her eyes. "I'm glad I wasn't alone," he said, then lifted his hand in a limp wave as the paramedics wheeled him away. Feeling touched and oddly comforted, Sadie walked slowly back towards the doors of the ER. The gash on her forehead was starting to ache, and a heavy fatigue was creeping in to every muscle in her body. Physically, she knew that she desperately needed to rest, but mentally she was desperate to get out and join in with the investigation into Masha Trent's disappearance. Every moment that she was sitting here was a wasted opportunity to be looking for the killer.

"I hate hospitals," the Deputy said next to her. "It's that smell, you know? Like bleach."

"Yeah," Sadie said, pausing to look around at the busy ER waiting room. "I know what you mean." The place didn't seem to have changed one bit from when she was a child. Like most kids, she and Jessica had had their fair share of bumps and scrapes. It had always been her mother who had accompanied them, she remembered. After she had passed, when Sadie had fallen from her bike and broken her arm at the age of thirteen, she had to bring herself. Her father had been too drunk to drive.

"Sadie? Sadie Price?" A doctor walked over to them with an expression of surprised recognition. Sadie smiled as she remembered him. Although older, with a white rather than red beard, she recognized Doctor O'Malley, who more often than not had been the one to patch up those bumps and scrapes.

"Doctor. How nice to see you," Sadie said, feeling an affectionate warmth for the old medic. This was one face from the past that she didn't mind seeing.

His brow creased with concern as he saw the cut on her head. "Are you okay?"

Sadie nodded. "It's pretty minor," she assured him.

"It's good to see you back in town," the doctor said, then he looked embarrassed. "Not under the circumstances, though, of course," he said hastily. "It must have been terrible news."

Sadie felt confused. He didn't seem to be referring to the murders.

"I'm not sure what you mean?"

The doctor's face went as white as his beard as he looked at her uniform and realized his mistake. "You don't know? About your father?"

Sadie shook her head numbly. Next to her the Deputy looked from one to the other and then walked quickly towards the doors. "I'll wait for you in the trawler, Price," she said, diplomatically leaving them to talk.

"What's wrong with my father?" Sadie asked. Her mouth felt dry. The doctor laid a hand gently on her elbow, gesturing for her to move into the corner, where they wouldn't be overheard. Sadie's head started to thump again with pain.

"I'm so sorry Sadie," Doctor O'Malley said in hushed tones. "But your father has stage four lung cancer. Have you not seen him?"

"No," Sadie said. She felt nothing at the doctor's words, but then what he was telling her didn't seem real. Her father was tough and hard, even with the alcoholism. He had never been sick that she could remember. She couldn't imagine him so ill.

"You might want to," the doctor said, his eyes full of compassion. "He may not have long…his prognosis wasn't good."

Sadie couldn't speak. Her mind scrambled around for a coherent reply, but there seemed to be nothing to say, or if there was then she couldn't find the words. She hated her father. Didn't she? Or after all this time, perhaps he simply meant nothing to her. And yet, she could feel the shock of the news, and had an overwhelming urge to cry. Perhaps she would have done, but Doctor O'Malley's beeper went off, making her jump.

"I'm sorry, Sadie," he said, already turning away from her. "I have to go." He rushed off, leaving Sadie staring after his back.

The news swirled around in her consciousness, her mind struggling to get a grip on it. She couldn't think about this right now. Taking a deep breath, Sadie walked out of the hospital and headed back towards the trawler.

As she walked through the revolving doors, Sadie was so lost in her thoughts that she nearly walked headfirst into a woman and a teenage girl who were entering the ER. The girl was clutching an injured arm to her chest and the mother looked panicked.

"I'm so sorry, ma'am," Sadie said, stepping aside to let them past. As they walked by her, the girl's long, dark hair and olive skin caught Sadie's eye and she felt her stomach jolt as she thought simultaneously of both Jessica and Masha, the missing girl. She thought of Masha's parents and the desperation that they must be feeling as they searched for their daughter, knowing that if she had simply wandered off then she would have been caught in the storm. This level of cold could kill quickly.

But the alternative, Sadie thought as she remembered the bloated corpses of Verity and Eva, was surely worse.

Unless there was a chance that Masha was still alive.

Sadie stood still, watching through the glass as a thought began to worry at the edges of her consciousness. She watched as the mother walked to the water dispenser to fetch her injured child a drink, her heels clacking on the floor. She was wearing red heeled boots that were so impractical for the current conditions that Sadie almost rolled her eyes, but the sight jolted something in her. The cherry red color of the woman's footwear reminded her of the dress and shoes that Eva had been wearing.

Or shoe. The other one had yet to turn up. Assuming it hadn't indeed been kept by the killer as a trophy, it was no doubt at the bottom of one of the Lynx lakes, having been pulled by the currents in a different direction to the body of its owner.

Pulled by the currents. Suddenly, Sadie remembered the conversation that she had been having with Sheriff Cooper before they had crashed. That if they could map the currents, then they might be able to figure out where the victims were being drowned and dumped, or at the very least, the direction that they had travelled in.

Now, with Masha missing and possibly about to suffer the same fate, it was even more urgent.

Turning away, Sadie went back to the trawler as fast as they could through the still thickening snow.

"Everything alright?" the Deputy asked as she clambered into the cab and belted herself in. "You look like you've seen a ghost."

"We need to go back to the station," Sadie said. Her heart pounded in her chest as her adrenaline rose again. Jane Cooper frowned.

"There will be a search party sent out now that the storm has passed," the Deputy told her. For once, there was a softness in her voice when she spoke to Sadie. "You need to get yourself checked out."

Sadie shook her head stubbornly. "We need to look for Masha," she said. The other woman looked at her as though she had gone insane.

"You need to rest, and it's getting late. Even without the storm, there isn't much of anything that we can do tonight."

"I think there might be," Sadie said. "I think I know how we can find the killer."

CHAPTER TWENTY FOUR

Sadie breathed a sigh of relief as the Deputy stared at her, and then gave a curt nod.

"Okay," she said, "let's go."

Without needing to be told, Mac started the engine. As he started to plow through the snow once again, Sadie stared through the window, thinking of Masha Trent. She was out there somewhere, no doubt terrified and possibly hurt. Without knowing why, Sadie felt as sure that the girl was still alive as she did that Masha was about to become their killer's third victim.

Or fourth?

Jessica's face swam into her mind again. She had been the same age as Masha had when she had been killed. Sadie was becoming more and more convinced that she was hunting her sister's killer as well as the more recent victims'. She swallowed down the cold rage that rose in her chest and willed Mac to move more quickly through the snow. Once they were alone at the station, she could tell the Deputy her theory.

They passed the saloon, and Sadie was shocked to see the lights were on. Everywhere else was dark and deathly quiet as the locals hunkered down against the storm.

Sadie shook her head, feeling bemused. "Surely Caz wouldn't keep the place open today?"

Mac grinned, and it lit up his weather-beaten face. "Ah, Caz will always open up if there are customers," he said. "Some of the folks round here won't let a blizzard get in between them and their drink."

Sadie knew her father would be included in that group, even if, according to Ted, he preferred to drink alone in his cabin. She wondered briefly if his condition would have convinced him to give up the booze, but knowing how stubborn the old bastard could be, she doubted it.

They pulled up outside of the station, and Sadie and the Deputy jumped down from the cab.

“Shall I wait?” Mac called after them. Sadie stopped and looked up at the sky. The snow and wind had settled into a consistent rhythm now, and the storm looked as though it was here to stay for some time.

“We could be here a while,” the Deputy told him, sounding annoyed. She glanced at Sadie. “This had better be good, Price,” she murmured, low enough to be out of Mac’s earshot.

“Tell you what,” Mac said. “I’ll hang around town for a bit in case you officers need a lift anywhere.” He smacked his lips together. “After all this, I need a drink. Seems a shame not to take advantage of the saloon being open.”

“Thank you,” Sadie said, watching him drive away. If it wasn’t for the ice harvester and his snowplow, then she and the Sheriff would have frozen to death.

The Deputy opened up the otherwise empty station, and Sadie followed her into the office she had first seen the day before. The Deputy turned on the heater then went straight into the kitchenette to fill up her flask. Then she took a seat next to Sadie.

“Okay, so what’s your idea?” she asked bluntly. She looked as tired as Sadie herself, Sadie realized as she saw the other woman’s face had taken on a pinched look and there were dark shadows under her eyes. In spite of the initial hostilities, she felt a stab of sympathy for Deputy Cooper. She would have been on the Masha Trent case all afternoon and had just rescued her brother from near freezing. She had been up early too, raiding Peter Montgomery’s with them.

Sadie could hardly believe that the raid had been just that morning. It seemed a lifetime ago. So much had happened in the past two days that time had lost all meaning. She was exhausted beyond belief, but she also knew that there would be no sleep for her until they had found Masha Trent.

“Deputy,” Sadie said urgently, “do you know any locals who have extensive knowledge of the currents that connect the lakes and the gorge?”

Deputy Cooper looked confused, then shrugged. “Not really. Mac would be your best bet. There is certainly nothing that he doesn’t know about ice around here. If he doesn’t know, he would probably know someone who does.”

“Can you call him to come back? He won’t have gotten far yet.” Sadie was already standing up.

“Now?”

"I was talking about this with your brother earlier, before the crash," Sadie explained, her voice urgent. "The lakes are linked under the ice, right? That's why we don't know where Verity and Eva were actually drowned, because the current carries them."

"Right, of course" the Deputy said, looking concerned. "Are you sure you're feeling all right, Price? I mean, you have taken a knock."

"There has to be a pattern to the currents," Sadie continued, "Even if it changes with the seasons or weather or whatever, it should be at least somewhat predictable. We thought if we could get a map of the currents then it might give us an insight into where the girls were drowned."

"Okay, I understand that," the Deputy said, nodding slowly. "But it doesn't need to be investigated right now, does it? It sounds pretty technical."

"Listen," Sadie said impatiently, "if Masha has been taken by the same person who killed Verity and Eva – and I think we both know by now how incredibly likely that is – then if we can figure this out, there's a chance we might be able to locate, or intercept, the killer before it's too late. A small chance, perhaps, but it has to be worth a try. We might not have access to any technology right now, but local knowledge can go a long way."

Jane Cooper raised both eyebrows, and Sadie was expecting her to display her usual cutting sarcasm, but instead the Deputy nodded again. There was a hopeful look in her eyes, and for the first time Sadie considered that the other woman might just care about the murdered girls as much as she did. Finally, a look that was something approaching mutual respect passed between them.

"You're right. It might be a shot in the dark, but it can't hurt to try. I'll call Mac. We can use the computer here and see what we can do. The National Oceanic and Atmospheric Administration department website should be some help, and Mac should be able to interpret the data." The Deputy sounded excited as she pulled out her phone to call the ice harvester.

"Damn it, I'm struggling to get a signal," she said, exasperated as the phone refused to connect. "Let me try in the back room."

Sadie waited, her heart in her throat. The more that she thought about it, the more that she was certain this could be a huge breakthrough. It was something that would have been done at some point, she was sure, but Masha's disappearance meant that they had no time to wait for other experts to get involved. Verity had been seen at most a few days before turning up dead. With no time of death, they had no way of knowing if the killer had kept her or killed her straight away.

Which meant that Masha Trent was running out of time. This had to work, Sadie thought, anxiety pooling in the pit of her stomach. It had to.

Deputy Cooper came back into the room, looking pleased, and at the sight of her expression Sadie gave a sigh of relief. "You got through?"

"Yes, he's on his way back now. He had barely gotten down the road; there's a huge snowbank."

While they waited the Deputy fired up the computer on the desk, which looked as though it had seen better days, with a chunky monitor and matching tower. It reminded Sadie of IT class at school. They had never been able to get internet back then, but then in those days it was considered to be for nerds only. Now, it could prove to be a lifesaving tool.

Except, the internet signal wasn't working either. Deputy Cooper banged her hand on the table in frustration just as Mac knocked at the station door.

"I'll let him in. Keep trying," Sadie urged. She let the old man in and led him through into the office.

"We're trying to access the NOAA database," she explained. "If we could map the currents under the ice, we might be able to track what direction the bodies have moved around in. Is there a chance that we could work back from that and figure out where they were originally drowned?"

Mac looked thoughtful; his head tipped to one side like a buzzard. "Yes," he said, "I'd say there's a good chance. I can't guarantee complete accuracy, but there's few folks around here who knows as much about the lakes as I do." He looked proud of himself, and Sadie couldn't help but grin.

Her face fell as she heard the Deputy curse behind her. "It's no good," she wailed, "I'm not going to be able to connect."

Sadie felt a moment's despair, then Mac said, "Looks like we're going to the saloon after all." She raised her eyebrows at him.

"A drink is the last thing I feel like."

Mac shook his head. "Not for booze. Caz's laptop. She has the best Wi-Fi signal for miles around. We all go to her when our signals are failing, and we need something."

Sadie was already on her way out of the door.

CHAPTER TWENTY FIVE

Sadie was surprised to see that Mac was right, and there were two old men already in the bar, playing dominoes at a table in the corner. She wondered if they would be here for the duration of the storm.

There was a welcome open fire roaring at the back of the room and Sadie stopped to warm her hands on it as the Deputy and Mac walked over to the bar to ask Caz about using her laptop. She stared at the flames, willing her mind to go blank of everything but the possibility of finding the information they needed.

To think of anything, in fact, other than the words of the doctor. That bit of news was far more than she could process right now, and it still seemed surreal to her, as though she had imagined the whole conversation.

“Price,” Deputy Cooper called to her. Sadie joined them at the bar. Caz looked up from powering up her laptop and smiled at her. Her eyes went to the cut on her head, but she didn’t ask the question that must have been on her lips, inquiring where she had obtained it. Sadie knew that most people would have asked.

She decided that she liked Caz.

“Okay,” the bar owner said, spinning the laptop around to face them. “Here you go. The signal’s working and you’re all ready to Google. It might be intermittent, but it always comes back on. I’ve used it through worse storms than this. Sometimes it’s the only thing that does work; God knows my television reception here is terrible.”

Sadie smiled politely, but her attention was on the screen as she located the website that she needed.

The National Oceanic and Atmospheric Administration website popped up in front of her without delay, and the three of them sighed with relief. Sadie scrolled through until she found what she was looking for. The ‘tides and currents’ page for Alaska, with a long list of locations, pressure measurements, altitudes and coordinates that looked like gobbledy-gook to Sadie, but would hopefully mean something more significant to Mac. She slid the laptop over to him.

His hooded eyes peered at the screen, saying nothing. The Deputy fidgeted impatiently on her stool.

"So, what do you think, Mac," she demanded. "Can you do it or not?"

Mac nodded slowly. "Get me a pen and paper," he said brusquely, "and I can use this to chart the gorge."

"Don't you want to make a chart, or something?" Caz asked, staring at the list of numbers and looking as baffled by them as Sadie felt.

Mac shook his head. "This is enough technology for me," he said. "I'm old school."

Caz rooted around under the bar and passed him a memo pad and pencil. It looked as though she had been chewing on the end. Mac didn't seem to notice; however, he was engrossed in the measurements. After a while, he sketched what looked to be a crude map of the Lynx lakes and the gorge.

"So, the first body, you found here, right?" he asked, tapping the pad. The deputy took the pencil from him and drew a large 'X' on the lake where Tom Willoughby had found Verity. Then she drew another one on the lake near the gorge, where Eva had been found. Mac nodded and went back to the screen and then the pad, scribbling down measurements in various places.

"Okay," he said after a while, drawing a line of the map with his finger, "so, are you assuming this guy threw them in at the same place?"

"Potentially," Sadie said, erring on the side of caution, while the Deputy simultaneously said "Yes," and then added, sounding excited, "Have you figured something out?"

"Well," Mac said slowly, "as I said, I can't give you any guarantees, but I reckon I'm near as right."

"Go on," Sadie urged.

"Well, you see these patterns here?" Mac asked, tapping a row of figures. Sadie had no idea what they meant.

"I haven't been in Alaska since I was a kid," she confided. "My knowledge of the local currents is about as good as my night vision. Can you break it down for me?"

Mac looked pleased, his face lit up like a little kid, and Sadie guessed that he rarely had the chance to indulge his passions for ice and currents with anyone who wanted to listen. Now he had Sadie, Deputy Cooper and Caz hanging off his every word. She wondered how often it was that he had this much company. Being an ice harvester in Alaska must be a pretty lonely profession.

"These show the direction and speed of the currents, and they have been pretty steady for the past few days," he said. "So, my best guess is that this body," he tapped on the first 'X,' was dumped before the other girl was."

Sadie and the Deputy exchanged a glance. So, Verity had been killed – or at least, her body disposed of – before Eva, in the same order that the girls had been found. Sadie wondered if Eva had still been alive when Verity had been found. If there had ever been any chance of saving her.

It was too late for Eva now, but it didn't have to be too late for Masha.

Sadie leaned forward, staring at Mac's roughly drawn map, the squiggles taking shape in front of her.

"So, can you take a guess as to where they were originally drowned?" she asked.

"Better than a guess," he said proudly. "The only place that they could realistically have been dumped, given the direction of the current and the need to not be seen, is this lake here." He tapped a smaller circle on his map, this time a good way behind the gorge. Sadie frowned, trying to picture the location in her mind.

"Wouldn't that be in the pine groves, at the bottom of the mountain range?" she said. Mac looked surprised at her knowledge of the place.

"Yes, that's where it is," he confirmed. "You know it?"

"I never knew there was a lake there," Sadie said, "But I spent plenty of time as a teenager messing around in the pines nearby."

With Jessica, she thought. And Matthew too, and a few other friends. Not that they had ever dared to go too far, which was no doubt why they had never found the lake that Mac mentioned. A school friend, Brian, had taken them there to show them the survivalist lair that his father, an enthusiastic trapper, had set up. He had shown them where all of the traps were, and they had great fun scaring each other, until Matthew had very nearly blundered into and set off one of the smaller traps. She could still remember how white he had gone when he had realized he had come within a hair's breadth of losing his foot.

That was the last time she had been up there. She wondered if the traps were still there.

"I know it," Deputy Cooper said. "It's not too far past the gorge, if you wanted to take a drive up there now?" She looked at Sadie and then at Mac, who looked dubious.

"In this storm? I don't think anyone would be out in this, do you? Even a killer," he laughed nervously, as though he had just realized exactly what he had gotten himself into.

The Deputy's radio crackled suddenly, and she slid off her stool and walked across the bar to answer it, speaking in hushed tones. Sadie wondered if it was about the Sheriff and felt a stab of anxiety. There had been a moment in the snowcat when she had really thought that she and Logan Cooper were going to freeze to death together.

"The search party for Masha has disbanded," the Deputy informed her as she returned. "They didn't find anything, but they didn't go much out of Anchorage town."

"I'm surprised they stayed out this long in this storm," Sadie said. She thought of the girl's parents, braving the worst elements for a futile search. Then she looked at Mac.

"If you don't want to take us – and I completely understand – could we please borrow your snowplow?" she asked. Even if it was a long shot that they could catch the killer in the act, they might find something of use at the lake in the trees. Something to lead them to Masha or her abductor.

Mac sighed but stiffened his shoulders.

"I'll take you. Can't have two women going up there on your own. Folks will talk."

Sadie saw the Deputy roll her eyes even as she jumped down from her stool.

"I'm so glad you'll be there to protect us," she said. "Let's go."

CHAPTER TWENTY SIX

Sadie stared out of the window as Mac drove, deep in thought. Anticipation of what they might find gnawed at her gut. She wasn't sure what would feel worse – to find Masha dead, or to discover nothing and be no closer to solving anything.

The pines came into view as they passed the gorge, along with Eddie Kolit's old shack and the road that led to the preacher's gated house. If their attempt to figure out where the killings were happening was accurate, then both men had easy access to the spot, and were likely to know about the quiet and little used lake. Eddie in particular. He may well have set some traps of his own.

"Mac," she said, turning away from the window, "when we brought the ice block to you yesterday, you mentioned that there was a trapper round here?"

Mac nodded. "Yeah, we just passed his cabin. Was he any use?"

"He was…interesting," Sadie said carefully. "He goes by the name of Eddie Kolit. Is there anymore that you can tell us about him? You already mentioned that he resented outsiders."

Mac furrowed his already creased brow, as though thinking hard.

"I don't know him too well," he said eventually. "Truth be told, I haven't seen him around for a while."

That corroborated the fact that the cabin by the gorge seemed abandoned, as well as what Eddie himself had told Sadie and the Sheriff earlier in the day. But that didn't mean he wasn't still using it…in fact, it would be the perfect place to hide missing girls.

"Why do you ask?" Mac said astutely. "Do you think it was him? When I said he was an unfriendly guy, that's not quite what I meant." Mac chuckled drily.

Sadie exchanged a glance with Deputy Cooper. Mac already now knew way more about this case than a civilian should, but there was no denying that without him and his knowledge of the ice and currents, they would still be running around chasing their tails. Eva's body would still be underwater nearby, and Yura would still be waiting for her to come home for the holidays, oblivious of her daughter's fate.

“We’re not at liberty to discuss those details, Mac; you know that,” the Deputy said, although in a good-natured way. Mac looked disappointed.

“Anything you can remember about Eddie, though, that seems off, it would be really helpful,” Sadie added.

“I’ll have a think,” Mac assured her, without taking his eyes off the track ahead.

Not that it could really be called a track, as any attempt at a path was long covered by the storm. As they rumbled past the gorge, an expanse of white greeted them. Even the pines were covered, making them look like huge, sparkly Christmas trees. Deceptively pretty, Sadie thought.

“It always gets to me,” Deputy Cooper said, picking up on Sadie’s own thoughts. “How beautiful the landscape here looks, just as it is at its most deadly.”

“It’s beautiful,” Mac said, with a note of longing in his voice that seemed out of character with the persona the brusque old man had so far presented. “Midwinter is my favorite time of year. Of course, it’s Christmas soon too. The birth of our Lord.”

Sadie felt surprised. Somehow, Mac hadn’t struck her as the religious type.

She wondered what church he went to.

Then Mac spoke again, and she knew exactly where he went to worship.

“It just looks so *clean*,” he said, almost wonderingly. “As though the earth itself is being purified and cleansed.”

Purified and cleansed. She had heard those words just this morning. Sadie glanced at the Deputy, trying to catch her eye, but Jane Cooper was looking out of the window too, not paying very much attention to Mac. Sadie wondered if she was being overly anxious. It had been a very long and very tough day.

She swallowed and tried to keep her voice light as she said, in a tone that was too casual, “Reverend Sutcliffe lives just back there too, doesn’t he? Lovely house.”

“He’s my preacher,” Mac said proudly. “And a righteous man. People around here would do well to listen to him.”

“Sutcliffe?” Deputy Cooper frowned as she rejoined the conversation. “He’s a bit of a fundamentalist, don’t you think? The way he goes on, it doesn’t sound anything like the church I grew up in.”

Sadie shot her a look, and this time the Deputy met her gaze as Sadie stared at her, willing her to understand what she was thinking. To let Sadie question Mac. The other woman's eyes went wide, and she opened her mouth to speak but then closed it again. She went back to staring out of the window, but her body had gone tense, and Sadie could feel her, coiled like a spring in the seat next to her, in between her and Mac.

The atmosphere in the cab was suddenly heavy with anticipation. Sadie hoped that Mac wasn't picking up on it, but the old man's expression, as he maneuvered the snowplow through the trees, was just a touch too casual.

"Folks say that about him," he said, "but they're wrong. Too many churches try to be liberal these days." In spite of his countenance, there was a note of steel in his voice. A cold anger that sent a chill through Sadie as she heard it.

Beware the iceman. He will kill you all.

It seemed impossible that Mac could have anything to do with this, but the angry, hateful looking guy that she was talking to now seemed to bear no resemblance to the genial guy who had just been helping them with the location of the lake.

Or had he been stringing them along the whole time? Enjoying teasing them with the information that he had known all along? Now that she thought about it, he had been far too sure of the original location of the bodies. He had figured it out so quickly. Sadie had put it down to his extensive knowledge of the area, but perhaps it had been because he already knew.

"Tradition is definitely important," Sadie said, playing devil's advocate. "I can see why the locals would flock to him. He really cares about the people around here."

"Oh, he really does," Mac replied, sounding mollified. "He understands the importance of keeping a pure heart. Staying away from temptation."

"I understand he wasn't happy about the celebrations of Quviasukvik in town," Sadie said, trying to sound as though she approved of that opinion. To bait Mac into revealing just what he thought of 'temptations' and how to deal with them.

"Neither are most of us locals," Mac said, and face twisted with something resembling disgust. "This is a Christian country. Heathens should not be allowed to taint it with their pagan celebrations and customs. It's wrong. We shouldn't be expected to put up with it."

“Heathens?” Sadie said softly, watching him. His eyes seemed to blaze with sudden rage, and he was almost unrecognizable from the genial guy he had been just minutes before.

“Yes,” he spat, “heathens. Some of them convert, of course, but the rest….”

“What about the rest?” Sadie asked, holding her breath. She expected Mac to rein it in, to understand that he was incriminating himself, but Sadie’s comments had clearly touched a nerve and the veins in his forehead were bulging with indignation.

“Vermin,” he pronounced. “The women, especially. Flaunting themselves…”

Mac cut off mid-sentence, but his hands tightened on the steering wheel until his knuckles went white, no doubt finally realizing that he had gone too far and exposed himself.

“We’re nearly here,” he said, his voice tight.

“Let’s pull up and walk,” the Deputy suggested. “Just in case we alert anyone that we’re here.” Her eyes flickered to Sadie and back again, her hand just perceptibly hovering over her holster.

Mac nodded and the snowplow rumbled to a stop. Sadie took a deep breath as she opened the door, glad for the sudden, freezing blast of air that slapped her cheeks.

Behind her, Jane Cooper screamed, and Sadie whipped around, her hand on her gun, struggling to draw it from her holster in the cramped space without falling out of the cab. The Deputy slumped lifelessly towards her, the back of her head covered in blood, while Mac lunged again, a vicious looking claw hammer in his hand.

Time seemed to stand still as Sadie struggled with her holster strap and to get herself out from under the Deputy at the same time. Just as she pulled out her gun, Mac nailed her in the neck with the claw hammer, sending her tumbling backwards out into the snow, the Deputy on top of her, and Mac rearing up once again, about to deliver a second blow. Blood was shooting from her neck like a geyser, but she was barely aware of it. Her gun was flung from her hand, and she heard it clatter somewhere on the floor of the cab. Mac bent to look for it, giving Sadie the seconds that she needed to scramble out from under the Deputy. She wanted to check if Jane had a pulse, but there was no time.

She had to run.

Seeing her move, Mac discarded his search for her gun and jumped out of the cab after her in a surprisingly lithe move. He was a lot stronger – and faster – than he looked. His face was twisted with rage as came after her, the hammer raised above his head.

Sadie ran in the direction of the trees, pressing a hand to her neck to try and stem the flow of blood as she wondered just how long she had before she passed out from blood loss. Her heart pounded in her ears as she ran, and she could hear Mac coming after her.

As fit as the old man might be for his age, Sadie was a highly trained agent and in normal circumstances could have easily outrun him – even overpowered him. But even with the adrenalin pumping through her and masking the effects of the hammer blow, she knew that she was in trouble. She was losing far too much blood. It ran between her gloved fingers and in a warm flow over the back of her hand. Landing on the snow at her feet. A stream of crimson on white.

Sadie could feel the strength going from her legs, and her vision blurring. A wave of nausea threatened to overtake her, and she stumbled, before righting herself and driving her thighs forward as hard as she could, even as she knew it was hopeless. She could hear Mac's labored breathing behind her even through the blizzard and knew that he would be on her any minute.

She was going to die here. In the snow. She wondered briefly if he would dump her frozen body in the lakes. Like Verity and Eva.

Like Jessica.

Behind her, Mac howled above the storm. "You can't have her!" he shrieked. "She's mine! God brought her to me, so that I could keep her clean and pure, before she becomes corrupted like those whores. 'Suffer the children to come unto me…' Can't you see, I'm doing God's work!"

Through the creeping fog that threatened to eclipse her consciousness, Sadie realized that he was talking about Masha. And the way that he was talking…suggested that she could still be alive.

She could save her.

Sadie's head cleared and she felt a new surge of adrenaline rush through her, propelling her forward and out of Mac's reach. With a new clarity, she saw that she knew vaguely where she was. If she could just remember the way….

Then she realized that she couldn't hear Mac chasing her anymore.

But she could hear something else. An engine. Lights swept the snow in front of her.

Mac had gone back for the snowplow. They might not be the fastest of vehicles, but they were still faster than an injured human, even an FBI agent who had excelled at track.

Gathering every bit of strength and resolve she possessed, Sadie hurled herself forward. If she could just get off the tundra and into the pines, she would have a chance. Her blood was roaring in her ears and a painful cramp stabbed her side as she forced herself forwards. The lights from the snowplow came closer, but Sadie didn't dare to look back.

As she reached the edge of the trees, she sobbed with relief, but knew that she couldn't afford to slow.

She veered sharply off through the trees, knowing it would slow Mac down to have to turn among the pines. The gap between them was still too small however, and Sadie knew that she didn't have long before she either fell or Mac caught up with her. She couldn't allow that to happen.

She had to live.

She had to save Masha.

And she knew what she had to do.

CHAPTER TWENTY SEVEN

Sadie's chest burned as she ran, and her breath wheezed from her throat. She kept her eyes fixed resolutely ahead and her hand pressed to the wound in her neck, trying not to think about the amount of blood she must be losing. Behind her, the snowplow rumbled on, but the twists and turns through the trees were preventing it fromcatching her up. As the trees thickened, Sadie knew that Mac would have to get out and pursue her on foot again, which would hopefully buy her a few more precious seconds.

The trees closed in around her and she propelled herself forward as the lights from the plow died and she heard Mac jump out and come after her, howling with rage.

She heard the loud crack of a gun – probably her own – and ducked low, running through the trees almost at a crouch. A few more shots fired, one bullet whizzing perilously close to her ear. She counted them, sobbing with relief when she heard the last one.

Of course, he still had the claw hammer, and Sadie was unarmed.

Sort of.

It wasn't the lake that she was attempting to head towards. If Masha was there, then she was already dead. Instead, Sadie was desperately trying to remember the location of her school friend's old survivalist lair. The depths of the pines all looked the same, and she dug in her memory for landmarks that might lead the way. She was sure that she was at least heading in the right direction, but she needed to be accurate if her wild plan was going to work. Her chances were slim, she knew, but that was better than none.

Somewhere in the background, a wolf howled. The haunting noise startled her, drawing her attention in its direction, and her eyes fell on a twisted pine stump. A jolt of recognition ran through her.

It was here. Now she just needed to remember the lay out of the traps – and ensure that she didn't stumble into one herself. For a brief second, she closed her eyes, and let the years fall away.

She remembered the evenings that she had traipsed through here with a bunch of school friends as Brian showed off his father's traps.

Matty was often with her, and sometimes, Jessica too. Brian would urge them to move slowly, detailing where each trap was and explaining just how each one worked. She and Matty had been fascinated, and she had known this terrain like the back of her hand, just as she had most of the lakes. Alaska was the sort of place that claimed you, that got under your skin and never allowed you to truly leave. How could she have forgotten?

A vivid flashback of her, Jessica, Matty, and Brian creeping through the trees as they approached the biggest trap of all, the bear trap, came to her and Sadie allowed herself a smile as she remembered how Jessica had clutched her arm. To protect Sadie, she had said, but Sadie knew it had been more to reassure herself.

Now, Sadie let those memories guide her, even as her thighs began to tremble with the effort that they could no longer keep up. She heard Mac close behind her, gaining on her fast. Too fast. Just a few more meters were all she needed.

Sadie knew that she had one shot at this and that she had to time it perfectly. Too soon and she would be the one in the trap. Too late and her one chance of survival would be lost.

Mac was right behind her now, so close that she could hear him panting. She had a matter of seconds before he reached her.

She saw the large cluster of three pines together that she was looking for and started to count her strides. One…two…three…

…now.

Sadie suddenly ducked down and rolled sharply to the left, too quickly for Mac to realize at first what she was doing, and so he blundered on for a few steps before trying to turn after her. For a horrible moment, Sadie thought that her plan hadn't worked, and she had nothing left, no energy in her aching body to fight with.

Then she heard the sound of the trap, Mac's agonized scream, and the sickening crunching, squelching sound as the wooden spike of the bear trap impaled Mac through the center of his chest.

Sadie dragged herself to her feet, gasping for breath, and slowly turned to face Mac.

The wooden spike stuck out of the center of his chest, lifting him off his feet so that he dangled in the air. Not yet dead, his breath was coming in gurgles, and he coughed blood up as his eyes fixed Sadie with a mixture of shock and rage.

"Where is Masha?" she demanded. Although the state of the old man was pitiful, Sadie couldn't muster any sympathy for him. He was a killer, and would happily have killed her, too.

Mac shook his head, even though the movement must have caused him severe pain, and in spite of his agony his bloody lips managed to curl into some semblance of a sneer. Sadie resisted the urge to scream at him and to demand that he tell her where the girl was and whether or not she was still alive. She refused to let him die with that last satisfaction.

Instead, she leaned her weight on the end of the wooden stake. Mac screamed, long and hard, his pain echoing through the trees. Up in the mountains, the wolf howled in response.

"I'll ask you again," Sadie said through gritted teeth, "where is Masha? Is she alive?"

Mac glared at her and coughed up a glob of blood. She was losing him.

"Yes," he wheezed, "she's alive…my shop…outhouse."

Sadie nodded curtly. "And the others? You killed them?"

Mac's eyes blazed with fire, and Sadie saw the madness in them. Under his genial, bluff old boy persona, it seemed Mac had been a true madman.

"Whores," he spat, his hatred tangible. Sadie took it as a confession. She turned away, gathering the last reserves of her strength to make her way back to the snowplow.

"Don't…leave me…here," he gasped behind her. Sadie turned to him, and her final question, the one she hardly dared to ask, came to her lips.

"Did you kill Jessica?" she asked. When he didn't reply, she asked again, reaching for the stake. "Jessica Price. My sister. She was seventeen. She died fifteen years ago, drowned in the same lakes as the others. Did. You. Kill. Her?" Sadie rapped out the last words, glaring at Mac now with a righteous anger to match his own when she saw realization dawn in his eyes.

He recognized her sister's name. Sadie held her breath as his lips moved and he tried to speak again, but only bubbles of blood came out.

"Tell me!" Sadie demanded. "Tell me, Mac!"

His eyes were starting to glaze over. Then, just as death spasms started to rack his body, he spoke again through a gurgle of blood.

"Not…me," he rasped. "Ask…your father."

Then his head rolled back, and he died before Sadie could question him any further.

CHAPTER TWENTY EIGHT

Sadie hauled herself back into the snowplow with difficulty, her own breath ragged and wheezing now, each inhale making her neck throb more. She reached for the rearview mirror and turned the interior light on and saw Deputy Cooper slumped in the seat next to her. The wound in her head was clumped with dried blood but looked as though it may not be fatal.

Sadie reached for her to check for a pulse, jumping when the Deputy jolted, and her eyes flickered open. She looked around, her eyes unfocused and wandering.

"Jane," Sadie said softly, "It's me, Agent Price. Can you hear me? You're safe. I'm going to get you some help."

Jane Cooper blinked heavily as she tried to focus on Sadie. As her consciousness returned, she suddenly looked panicked.

"Mac!" She gasped, trying to grab Sadie's arm. Sadie patted her hand soothingly. "It's okay, Jane. Mac's gone."

"He's the killer," Jane told her, her pupils wide.

"I know," Sadie assured her. "It's okay. He's gone."

Jane looked relieved and closed her eyes, but then they flew open again.

"The girl? Masha?"

"I'm going to try and find her now," Sadie told her. "As soon as I can get a signal, I'm going to call an ambulance to get your head seen to, and then I'm going to find Masha."

Sadie spoke with more confidence than she felt, hoping that Mac hadn't been lying to her just to make her stop leaning on the stake. Or that Masha hadn't died in the interim. She dreaded to think what kind of state the poor girl might be in.

Before she set off, Sadie unzipped her ski jacket and tore off a piece of her shirt, tying it tightly around her neck. The bleeding had slowed a little, but she knew that it needed seeing to, and fast, or she would bleed out. Only the adrenalin and determination to find Masha was keeping her going.

Sadie started the engine, and the lights swept the pines. She could see her own blood trail in front of her, though it was starting to disappear under the still falling snow.

She wondered how long it would be before it had covered Mac's impaled body, and then pushed the macabre thought from her mind. She refused to feel bad about the man's death. She had been left with no choice. Mac would have killed her and Jane, and then gone back for Masha.

Sadie had chosen to survive.

As she drove, Jane moaned lightly in the seat next to her, and Sadie cast a worried eye over the other woman. She needed to stay awake but was drifting in and out of consciousness. With one hand Sadie tried her radio, but her signal was gone. She stepped full down on the gas pedal, willing the snowplow forwards.

She tried to keep her mind purely focused on finding Masha, but every time she thought of the girl, whom she had never seen, she thought of Jessica's face instead. For a moment, running towards the traps, she had almost felt Jessica with her. Sadie's eyes filled with tears.

Mac's last words echoed in her head on a loop. Like a stuck record that wouldn't turn off.

Ask your father…ask your father…

As much as she might want to believe that the ice harvester had been taunting her, Sadie instinctively felt that there was a truth at the heart of his words. If Mac knew her father, had maybe drank with him, then of course he would know all about Jessica. But even if that was the case, there had been more than simple malice behind his dying words. Sadie was sure of it. Yet, the implications of that were too horrible to bear.

Her father knew something about Jessica's death, and had never a breathed a word?

Or worse, he had caused Jessica's death.

Had he killed her?

Sadie shook her head, unable to bear the stab of grief that came with the thought. She loathed her father, he was a nasty, violent bastard and she wouldn't put it past him to be able to kill, but Jessica? She had been his favorite. It had always been Sadie, after their mother had died, who bore the brunt of his wrath. She couldn't imagine him hurting Jessica.

But then, that was the problem with killers, as her experience had taught her. There were always people who knew them, who were so certain that they couldn't possibly have committed the crimes they were accused of. Who just couldn't imagine it being true.

Could it be possible, that all this time she had dreamed of bringing her sister's killer to justice, and all along he had been under her very nose? She shuddered at the possibility.

As the gorge swept into view and then Eddie Kolit's old shack, Sadie brought her thoughts back to Masha. She couldn't do anything about Mac's words right now, or confront her father, but she could find Masha. That was the whole reason that she was here.

Sadie tried the radio again, and this time she got through.

"Agent Price," she said, and told them where she was heading. "I have Deputy Cooper with me," she continued, "and we are both badly injured. I've hit an artery in my neck and I'm losing a lot of blood."

"Is Deputy Cooper conscious?" the State trooper on the other end asked. Sadie looked over at the other woman. Her head was lolling back on the seat and the wound on her head was bleeding. Her eyelids flickered and she murmured something incomprehensible.

"Barely," Sadie said. "I may have located Masha Trent also, so send enough medics for three people. And please," she said as wave of dizziness threatened to overwhelm her, "be as quick as you can." She hoped that she had timed it right so that the rescue team arrived at the ice harvester's shop around the same time as she did.

Because if they left it too late, then they might well arrive to find three dead bodies.

*

Sadie checked Jane's pulse one more time before she got out of the snowplow outside of Mac's shop. The Deputy didn't stir this time, but her pulse was still steady. There was no sign of an ambulance as yet, and Sadie hesitated to leave her, but finding Masha was the priority.

Sadie unbuckled Jane's gun from her holster and put it in her own – just in case she found more than she was bargaining for – and then left the engine on to try and keep the other woman warm. With her hand over her holster, she walked around the shop, looking for the outhouse that Mac had spoken of.

"Hello?" she called as she walked, hoping that if Masha was there then the girl could hear her. Only silence greeted her, a creeping, ominous silence that made her shiver. Even the howling of wind and wolf had quietened, as though the whole landscape held its breath.

Around the back of the shop were three small outhouses, ramshackle buildings made of corrugated iron. Sadie jogged to the first of the outhouses, wrenching open the door.

"Masha!" she called again, to no reply.

Inside, the outhouse was nothing but blocks of ice and harvesting tools. Sadie ran to the second only to find much of the same. She cursed Mac under her breath as she tried the final building.

If that old bastard lied to me, she thought, *I might never find her.*

"Masha!" she screamed again as she saw that the door to the third outhouse was firmly bolted. As Sadie raised her gun to shoot it open, she heard a whimper from inside.

"I'm coming," Sadie called. "Just hold on."

The padlock gave way and Sadie shoved her way inside, peering through the gloom. This one appeared empty, with no ice or tools catching her torch. For a moment Sadie thought she had imagined the sound, but then it came again, and her torch shone on a pile of tarpaulin in the far corner of the building. Running over to it, Sadie knelt down and lifted the tarp to see a girl huddled underneath.

"Masha," Sadie breathed. The girl's mouth was duct-taped and her hands and feet shackled. As Sadie reached for her, she felt the cold coming off the girl and knew that she had found her just in time. She untied her shackles as the girl watched her through huge eyes filled with tears and tried to rub some life back into her hands and feet before carefully removing the duct tape from her mouth.

The girl was shaking from hand to toes, eyeing Sadie with a mixture of relief and suspicion.

"You're going to be okay," Sadie told her. "There's an ambulance on the way."

"How did you know my name?" the girl said, her voice croaky. Sadie smiled gently.

"You've been reported missing," Sadie told her. "People are out there looking for you. We're going to get you back to your parents as quickly as we can. You're safe now Masha, I promise."

Masha smiled weakly back at her, but then her eyes filled with horror. For a second, Sadie thought that someone had crept in behind her – Tom Willoughby perhaps – but then she realized that Masha was staring at her neck.

"You're bleeding," the girl told her. "A lot."

Sadie pressed her hand to her neck, feeling a dull, throbbing pain as she did so. Weakness washed over her, and spots of black seemed to dance before her eyes. She shook her head fiercely.

"I'm fine, honestly," she reassured the girl, who didn't look convinced.

Outside, Sadie heard the wail of sirens.

"The ambulance is here," she murmured. She needed to help Masha get outside. She stood up, and as she did so the world seemed to spin, and her stomach flipped.

Then she was falling, and her cheek hit the cold floor just as everything went black.

CHAPTER TWENTY NINE

Where am I? Sadie blinked as she opened her eyes to be met with a harsh strip light and turned her head to the side.

Or at least, she tried to. There were heavy bandages around her neck, and she felt as though she was aching from head to toe. Her mouth was dry, and her head thumped with a tension headache.

She had been in better shape, that was for sure.

"Glad to see you awake. How are you feeling?" Sheriff Logan Cooper walked into her room, a smile on his face. He looked a lot better than the last time that Sadie had seen him. His head had a small bandage on it, but otherwise he looked his usual self.

"I'm in the hospital," Sadie said, feeling confused, before everything came back to her in a rush. She stared at the Sheriff.

"Please tell me Masha and Jane are okay," she said as Cooper took a seat next to her bed.

"Masha is with her parents. She's shaken and terrified, but physically fine. Just a few cuts and bruises, surface stuff only."

"And I'm fine too, thanks to you," the Deputy's voice came as she too entered the room, giving Sadie an almost shy smile, at complete odds with her usual combative attitude.

"I didn't do anything, really," Sadie protested weakly. She had just done her job. The admiration with which the Sheriff and his sister were looking at her was making her feel uncomfortable. She wasn't sure if the outright hostility hadn't been easier to manage.

"Sadie, you were brilliant," Cooper said firmly. "Jane has told me how you drew Mac out, and all but got him to confess. And then you went back for her and Masha even with a gaping hole in your neck. I'm so glad we had you on this case with us. Masha would be dead right now without you."

Feeling oddly vulnerable, Sadie had to fight not to cry. "Thank you," she murmured. His acceptance of her meant more than she would have expected.

"Yeah," Jane cut in, grinning at Sadie, "I suppose you're okay, for a Fed. I've met worse."

Sadie grinned back. That was about all the apology that she was ever going to get from Deputy Cooper, but it was enough.

"Has the storm stopped yet?" she asked, changing the subject. As much as the fuzzy warm feelings floating around the room were a welcome shift, she didn't like the feeling of vulnerability they promoted. "I need to check in with Golightly."

She still had so much to do.

Cooper shook his head. "You don't stop, do you?" he said, and Sadie couldn't tell if he was more exasperated or inspired by her. "No. Not as yet. The storm is still going, and currently all the phone lines are down, so we can't do much of anything. You probably won't want to stay here, I know. Myself and Jane have a few spare rooms that we often rent out to tourists. You're welcome to stay with us until this is over."

Sadie felt like crying at his kindness and blinked the threat of tears away. It must be the painkillers and the shock, she told herself. Seeing her expression, Cooper softened his voice.

"There's nothing you need to do right now, Price. You apprehended Mac and found Masha alive and well. Golightly managed to get a message through to the hospital earlier…he sounds impressed."

A nurse appeared, interrupting them, and the Coopers got to their feet. "We'll leave you be," the Sheriff said, "But I'm just outside if you need me. I've just been discharged, Jane too."

Sadie looked up at the nurse as they left. "Does that mean that I can go, too?"

The nurse, an older woman with a heavyset frame and short gray hair, tutted at her. "That's a nasty wound on your neck. You lost a lot of blood. I would imagine the doctors would want to keep you in for another night, just to be on the safe side."

"But then I might not be able to leave at all, the way this storm is going," Sadie said reasonably. "And you might need the bed; there could be lots of accidents in this weather. Wouldn't it make more sense to leave with the Sheriff?"

The nurse shook her head, but she looked amused. "I'll speak to the doctor," she promised. "Do you have somewhere to stay? Because like you said, with this storm, you won't make it back to Anchorage."

Sadie thought about the Sheriff's offer and smiled.

"I think so," she said.

*

Sadie walked out of the hospital with the Sheriff and Deputy Cooper. The snowplow was parked outside, and Sadie could barely suppress a shudder as she remembered the events of the night before.

It was early evening now and the sky was darkening again to a deep purple. The snow was falling steadily. Sadie tipped her head up and took a deep breath, ignoring the twinge of pain in her neck. The air felt fresh.

"Are you sure you will be okay to drive?" the Sheriff was saying to his sister as they climbed inside the vehicle. She ignored him, turning the keys in the ignition by way of answer. Logan reached a hand out to Sadie and helped her inside. Her legs felt weak, and as she sat down her stomach rumbled audibly.

"Sorry, I'm starving," she said. "I couldn't eat that slop in the hospital."

"We all are," the Deputy said. "I can't wait to get my feet up in front of the fire, to be honest. I feel as though I haven't been warm in years."

"Thank you for letting me stay," Sadie said to them both. "I really appreciate it. Would you mind if we made one stop on the way?"

The Sheriff searched her face, but in reply he only said "Sure."

They set off.

Sadie could hardly wait to get to the Cooper's place and enjoy a real fire and some hot food. The last few days felt like years, and just like Jane, she felt as though she had forgotten what home comforts were.

But there was just one thing that she had to do first.

CHAPTER THIRTY

As Sadie made her way up the drive, the snow fell around her in fluffy white flakes. The air was crisp and still, and it was as though the driving winds and blizzard of ice of yesterday had never been. Instead, the scenery around her was Christmas card perfect. Above her, a full moon hung low and swollen in the indigo sky.

It was the perfect setting for a reunion, but Sadie wasn't anticipating any kind of happy ending.

The cabin looked more dilapidated than she remembered. The fence around the porch was broken and the roof needed fixing. The green paint on the front door was peeling.

Otherwise, everything looked exactly as Sadie remembered. For a moment, she felt like a fifteen-year-old girl again.

But she wasn't. She was a grown woman, and it was time to confront her past. Sadie set her shoulders back, took a deep breath, and knocked firmly on the door.

"Who is it?" a raspy voice came from within. Sadie didn't reply, her voice suddenly freezing in her throat. He sounded older and weaker, but it was still him.

The door opened and he stood there, glaring at first to see who had disturbed him. Then his expression turned to one of shock.

"Sadie?"

Sadie nodded.

"Hello Dad," she said.

NOW AVAILABLE!

ONLY RAGE
(A Sadie Price FBI Suspense Thriller—Book 2)

ONLY RAGE (A Sadie Price FBI Suspense Thriller) is book #2 in a chilling new series by mystery and suspense author Rylie Dark, which begins with ONLY MURDER (book #1).

Special Agent Sadie Price, a 29-year-old rising star in the FBI's BAU unit, stuns her colleagues by requesting reassignment to the FBI's remote Alaskan field office. Back in her home state, a place she vowed she would never return, Sadie, running from a secret in her recent past and back into her old one, finds herself facing her demons—including her sister's unsolved murder—while assigned to hunt down a new serial killer.

FBI Special Agent Sadie Price has barely recovered from her last case when she is assigned to an urgent, new one: a gruesome discovery has revealed women are turning up dead, their bodies found in the cargo holds of fishing boats, half-eaten by crabs.

Sadie, stuck for the winter and here to stay, must form a tenuous alliance with Sheriff Logan Cooper and the local bar owner if she is to penetrate the icy wall of outcast locals. Exploring the harbor and the crusty workers who inhabit it, Sadie needs answers to this seemingly unsolvable string of murders—and to the mysteries of her own past.

Suspects abound in the remote and unforgiving landscape. But this is no garden variety killer, and hunting him down may end up a bridge too far even for a brilliant agent like Sadie. In a deadly game of cat and mouse, can Sadie prove herself a match for this killer?

Or will he prove to be her undoing?

An action-packed page-turner, the SADIE PRICE series is a riveting crime thriller, jammed with suspense, surprises and twists and turns that you won't see coming. It will have you fall in love with a brilliant and scarred new character, while challenging you, amidst a barren landscape, to solve an impenetrable crime.

Book #3 in the series—ONLY HIS—is now also available.

Rylie Dark

Debut author Rylie Dark is author of the SADIE PRICE FBI SUSPENSE THRILLER series, comprising three books (and counting) and the CARLY SEE FBI SUSPENSE THRILLER, comprising three books (and counting).

An avid reader and lifelong fan of the mystery and thriller genres, Rylie loves to hear from you, so please feel free to visit www.ryliedark.com to learn more and stay in touch.

BOOKS BY RYLIE DARK

SADI PRICE FBI SUSPENSE THRILLER
ONLY MURDER (Book #1)
ONLY RAGE (Book #2)
ONLY HIS (Book #3)

CARLY SEE FBI SUSPENSE THRILLER
NO WAY OUT (Book #1)
NO WAY BACK (Book #2)
NO WAY HOME (Book #3)

www.ingramcontent.com/pod-product-compliance
Lightning Source LLC
Chambersburg PA
CBHW030614310726
48979CB00003B/719